Sullivaı

by

Andy Clancy

ISBN: 978-1-326-50147-1

PublishNation
www.publishnation.co.uk

This book is dedicated to my wife Husnuye and our children Siobhan, Michael and Melanie; without whose enthusiasm and support this book could not be written. It is also dedicated to Gibraltar and the spirit of those who served in the "Great Siege".

"No man thinks more highly of them than I do; I love and honour the English troops; I know their virtues and their valour; I know they can achieve anything except impossibilities"

William Pitt – Earl of Chatham 1777

Sullivan's War

Prologue
Bunker Hill, Charlestown,
American Colonies, June 17, 1775

New England was beautiful; a beautiful land of rolling countryside, fields, forests, growing towns and so much free space to breathe and live, it was a land of opportunity for those who wanted it and Corporal Tom Sullivan had never been so happy in his life. Basic training in Dublin seemed a long time ago; the army had become his life as if anything he had ever done before never existed. Tom looked back out across the harbour from the city of Boston as his transport boat sailed towards the beach at Charlestown. Tom was one of 60 men of the Light Company of His Majesty's 39th Regiment of Foot crammed into the boat. There were many other transports bringing 2,500 redcoats to Charlestown to dislodge a force of Yankee colonial militia that had set up fortifications on two positions known locally as Breed's Hill and Bunker Hill.

As the transports pulled up on the shore at Molton's Point; Sergeant Major Riordan took out his pocket watch eying it, as he snapped it shut and put it back inside his tunic pocket he smiled and looked at the young soldiers gathered near him, "two o'clock let's see what the afternoon brings boys", the watching redcoats were too nervous and tense but looked at Riordan eagerly as platoon after platoon of redcoats jumped out of their transports splashing through the water towards dry land. "Keep those muskets in the air lads and your cartouches as well, we want you firing well today" bellowed Sergeant Major Riordan. Regimental drummers and fifes started playing forming up tunes on their instruments; each soldier recognised their own tunes and started to look where the musicians were next to their Corporals, Sergeants and officers. Very quickly a mass of redcoats started to form into platoons, companies and then regiments. Corporal Tom Sullivan shouted "no3 company on me", as he ran next to his drummer and fife, he looked at his soldiers they were anxious, excited but they were good lads he thought to himself, O'Connor, Cullen, Murtagh; all from Ireland and a long way from home.

They looked up the hill and there they were; the militia. "Oh Jesus", Tom thought, they were ready, sitting behind earthworks they were ducking down as cannon balls from the Royal Navy ships in the harbour bombarded their positions.

They could see the militia loading their muskets. Tom looked across to Sergeant Major Riordan, "I know Tom, I've had some days in the army but today will be a bastard". Tom said nothing he could see the men of no3 company were formed but looking up at the same activity by the militia. Major Kellet was close by, "now gentlemen, we know how it, is look to your men, they need you this day, they need us". Tom and Sergeant Major Riordan immediately snapped to attention "Sir". He was a good man Major Kellet, Tom thought to himself, he stood out among the other officers he cared for his men.

Tom could hear himself praying, "holy father, if I forget you this day, I beg thee not forget me".

To assemble 2,500 soldiers into formation was no easy task but within a short while the attacking force was ready. Then they were formed up and ready to go the Light Company was positioned in line.

"Sir, why have they not sent us out as skirmishers to harass the militia, we are the Light Company"? Tom asked Riordan.

"Keep your voice down Sullivan, I know lad; the word is the generals are angry after our noses were bloodied at Lexington and Concorde. They want to show the militia what British redcoats can do and finish this thing now before it becomes a full blown war".

"We'll find out soon enough how strong they are I suppose Sergeant", Tom sighed.

"Too much talk Tom, lead the men", when Sergeant Major Riordan called him by his first name Tom knew the man he looked up to was worried.

Then the order came, "the 39th will advance, by the centre quick march". Off they went in pace, it was a great sight to behold, drums and fifes playing the British Grenadiers. Tom was proud, "hold your lines men", they were his lads he would bring them through this day.

As the regiment marched up the hill, The Light Company was in the second line, behind the Grenadiers.

The attacking troops continued up the hill, they were getting closer and closer to the militia line, the bastards were holding their fire Tom thought to himself. Sporadic flashes of smoke from the militia lines, then he heard the first whoosh of musket balls flying, Tom gritted his teeth he knew the first volley was coming, he could see militia men in uniform, officers, slashing their swords downwards, this is it, he squinted, he gritted his teeth, crack, flames, smoke and then whoosh almost the whole line of Grenadiers in front of Tom's went down, some dead most screaming writhing in agony.

That volley had been devastating and had stopped the whole attack in its tracks. As men dressed forwards to fill the gaps of their fallen comrades the militia continued to fire at will. Before they could dress forward the men in the second line were being hit. For many of the redcoats it was their first time in battle and the experience was terrifying. There was no order given to halt, the columns of men couldn't move forward against a wall of lead musket balls that came from the militia lines.

Muskets were not rifled so the lead balls would fly everywhere once fired, a musket was notoriously inaccurate, soldiers were hit everywhere, arms, legs, chest, head, the wounds were awful. The second line dressed forward as they had been trained so many times to fill the gaps left by the casualties of the first volley. Even before they could get in line the militia were firing at will, the air was a sea of hot lead and many more redcoats fell. Officers ran forward to encourage the men to keep going but the musket balls didn't care; they fell dying as well.

Men were dropping all around Tom, a musket ball hit his cross belt buckle, winding him and knocking him backwards and onto his back, he could hardly breathe but he was still alive. He sat back up and crawled forward onto his knees trying to collect his musket; he still couldn't catch his breath, as he looked at the chaos, he felt as though he was in another world, his mind couldn't settle the scene of horror around him. Tom could hear Major Kellet shouting but couldn't see him, Sergeant Major Riordan was holding up a wounded Private Murtagh waving his sword forward at the enemy.

All discipline had completely gone, the once ordered lines of redcoats were now small groups of men firing off their muskets in panic, there was no one leading the attack, officers, Sergeants anyone with rank was falling, the Yankees were going out their way to hit them. He stood up, presented his musket at the militia lines and saw an officer standing on top of their sandbags waving his sword.

"I'll have you ya bastard "he thought to himself.

As he fired his musket he felt the burn on the right side of his face as the gunpowder in the frizzen ignited, then the thump of the musket butt into his right shoulder and bang!

He lifted his head to follow his shot and saw the militia officer throw his arms in the air losing the sword and topple back into the trench behind him as a large spurt of blood spat from his neck.

It was a good shot and Tom instinctively went to reload his musket, no formal drill this time, he pulled another cartridge from his cartouche, bit the top paper off the cartridge keeping the musket ball in his mouth, dropped some powder down the barrel and spat the musket ball down after it tapping the butt on the ground, dropped the remaining powder from the cartridge, presented at the militia lines and bang he fired! Tom was now in a blind killing rage and fired again; like any good redcoat could with the famed four shots a minute. Tom was aware of musket balls flying near him, grazing him, but he felt he had an invisible shield around him and didn't care whether he lived or died, alas for his comrades they were dying all around him.

Thud! On Tom's right, Private Cullen made a wheezing noise after the thump of a musket ball hit him square in the chest. As Cullen dropped his musket, he looked at Tom and made a gurgling noise with blood coming out of his mouth, he held his hand to his chest with blood pouring through his fingers, he then fell to his knees and tumbled forward dead. This was more than personal for Tom Sullivan; some of these men had been with him since they were recruits in Dublin, he was incensed he wanted to kill as many Yankees as possible.

Tom was in the thick of battle, he could hear himself shouting at the men in his Light Company," independent fire at will lads, pour it into them"!

Then he could hear someone shouting at him.

"Sullivan, Tom Sullivan, get back here you idiot you're on your own"!

It was Sergeant Major Riordan shouting, gesticulating at him, he was right; turning back he could see the Sergeant Major had pulled the remnants of the Light Company back with him. With Tom there was nothing but the dead and wounded. The nearest man wounded and alive was private O'Connor, lying on the ground holding a hand to his shoulder trying to stem the flow of blood pouring from a wound; Tom instinctively leaned down grabbed O'Connor by his cross belts and dragged him back down to the Sergeant Major.

Very quickly, the two men reached the Light Company survivors who were leaning exhausted on their muskets just out of range of the militia. As Tom let go of O'Connor into the hands of two stretcher bearers he suddenly felt dizzy and his knees buckled.

"I know Corporal, take a few deep breaths, just look at you, how are you still alive"? Sergeant Major Riordan put his arm around Tom to steady him looking him up and down.

As well as the indentation of the musket ball on his cross belt buckle, Tom had wounds to his right soldier and left leg where he had been grazed by militia musket balls. Tom's chest was killing him where he had been hit earlier; as he tried to control his breathing Major Kellet appeared.

"39th Foot on me, we will reform for the next assault".

It wasn't just the 39th in trouble; across the line the whole attack was in complete chaos, without even firing a proper volley in return the first assault had failed and as the redcoats fell back down the hill they left countless numbers of their comrades dead and wounded lying where they fell.

The scene at the foot of the hill where the attacking force regrouped was like nothing Tom thought he would ever see. There were so many wounded; those who could manage to get back down the hill found that there were not enough stretcher bearers.

What started as an operation resembling a fine military parade became a scene of complete chaos; normally aloof generals were on foot pulling officers and soldiers together berating them. Tom had never seen so many dead officers, 2nd Lieutenants and Sergeants were organising and preparing to lead regiments. Casualties were so high that companies and even regiments were being pulled together to make ready for the next assault.

Things were going badly wrong and every soldier knew it, they had never expected the militia to be so belligerent.

As the survivors of the first attack reorganised themselves, more reinforcements arrived on transports from Boston, Marines and other line regiments. As their officers formed them up it was plain to see the unease on their faces as they saw the battered troops of the first assault reorganising themselves.

Tom had been in the colonies long enough to recognise the generals that led them. General Clinton was there; convincing wounded redcoats that could still stand to pick up muskets and join the next attack. Even General Howe, the commander of British forces in America was there, his sword out of its scabbard waving it above his head, "I'm joining you men we will take this hill and win this battle together! There was a cheer from the many soldiers standing near him. Despite the horror around him Tom almost smiled and thought, "If it takes General Howe to lead the next attack we must be in trouble"!

The Generals had worked hard and shown their worth, as the troops lined up again in column there was a renewed determination to take the hill but this time would be different! The Generals had gone into conference with the regimental officers, as the meeting broke up Major Kellet shouted.

"Sergeant Major Riordan, Corporal Sullivan, get over here now"!

As both men listened Major Kellet had clear instructions.

"Gentlemen, the main assault will still go in from the front, thanks be to god we won't be part of it. While the assault troops keep them busy, we will take the Light Company to the right and attack the militia left flank and take these damn Yankee positions once and for all. Once we get around that flank I want volleys poured into them then we break ranks and charge to the first set of earthworks and hit em hard. The Yankees fear our bayonets so put it to them, no pity no quarter they killed too many of ours for that, questions? No, then to your duties, no marching we go at the double"?

Soon enough order was restored; a new attacking formation was made up of the survivors and wounded of the first assault and the fresh reinforcements from Boston. General Howe and General Clinton at the front, both men were walking up and down the lines encouraging the soldiers, "You're the best soldiers in the British Army, I am proud of you, you will keep your discipline, listen to your officers, you will fire your volleys as only you can and then we will charge as one".

Soldiers were cheering again, especially those who had been in the first assault. The order was given to advance and the reformed brigade marched up Bunker Hill again to take the militia positions. As they marched up the hill again they could see it was covered in the bodies of dead and wounded redcoats.

The militia behind their earthworks had ceased all their firing and were obviously preparing their muskets to deliver more murderous volleys into the advancing redcoats; but this attack was different!

The whole Brigade halted barely within range of the militia lines, the militia officers realised what was happening and started to shout orders for their men to hurry loading their muskets and fire. Shots rang out from the militia and redcoats started to drop but this time their discipline was solid as a rock.

The order went along the whole attacking line, "make ready, present, fire!

A thousand muskets fired at almost the same time sending a volley of lead that sent the militia flying back into their trenches with the others ducking down behind their earthworks, this was how redcoats fought at their best, together in formation in a good old fashioned fire fight!

Some militia foolishly got up to fire thinking they were safe and were met by the second redcoat volley and more died before they could even level their muskets.

Then the redcoats used one of their oldest tactics honed through many years of war with the French; each regiment started firing by platoon, the militia didn't know what had hit them as this gave an almost constant field of fire from one end of the attacking lines to the other.

This was the opportunity that Major Kellet and the Light Company were waiting for; he shouted, "Right lads the heavy infantry are keeping them busy now follow me at the double"!

At that forty men started running behind the attacking columns to the right, all Tom could see was the backs of the men in front, smoke and the sound of musket volleys again. As Tom ran he couldn't feel his wounds or the breathlessness of running up and around a hill, his only thoughts were vengeance he wanted to get into those Yankee trenches and stick his bayonet in the first person he saw.

As the Light Company wheeled around the enemy left flank their numbers became very visible. Soon militia officers were shouting and men were leaving their posts from the frontal assault and taking up position opposite the approaching Light Company. Before they could form the militia started firing.

Major Kellet jumped up in the air and started hopping holding his right foot then fell over; a musket ball had hit the bottom of his boot, "damn it, damn it", he shouted in pain.

Sergeant Major Riordan went to the Major, "I can't run Sergeant Major but I'm alive, take the men forward and storm those bloody positions now"!

Before the Sergeant Major could answer the militia got a proper volley off, soldiers were hit as was Riordan and he flew backwards as if caught by a punch in the stomach.

Sergeant Major Riordan was a determined man and rolled himself upwards sitting on the ground, holding his hand over a musket wound on his lower stomach, he was near death, all around Tom men were falling but he went back to Riordan.

"Tom, get the men together and lead them it's all on you now".

"Yes Sir"!

His work done Riordan went even more white and looked at Tom, "oh Jesus" he muttered as though his wound was just an annoyance and then rolled forward dead.

Tom was not going to relive the horror of the first attack he was leading the Light Company now, as well as dead and wounded redcoats there were muskets and equipment lying everywhere, Tom shouted at the men, "no more marching, follow me running and grab an extra musket, do it now, I want them both loaded"!

The Light Company got in position adjacent to the militia left flank Tom bellowed, "all of you down on the ground and tap load your muskets".

The men didn't need a second command; on the ground they were safe from the militia fire. Loading a Brown Bess musket lying down was no easy task but the men went about their work with Tom crawling up and down their position checking to see that each man had two muskets loaded and primed.

"All stand" the whole company got to their feet.

"Make ready, present, fire"!

At last they got off a good volley, it hit the militia flank and they weren't expecting it, the musket balls sent bodies falling backwards writhing in agony, it was their turn to feel the pain!

Before the militia could return fire the men of the Light Company had dropped their empty muskets and picked up their second loaded ones. Tom shouted the same orders and hit the militia with another volley within seconds of the first, more of them went down.

This was the time, no more volleys, no more formations, Tom screamed his orders, "charge your bayonets"!

As one the men shouted,"huzzah"! As they pointed their bayoneted muskets towards the enemy.

"Now we put the bayonet to them lads, charge"! Tom ordered.

The screams of the Light Company as they charged were terrifying for the militia behind the earthworks, a few fired off their muskets in panic but many instinctively got up from their positions and staggered back in anticipation of meeting the fury of the redcoat charge.

As the Light Company charge went forward, Tom could hear the din of battle to his left as the main force charged the militia positions at the same time. In no time they were over the earthworks and on top of the militia; they had the killing frenzy having lost so many of their comrades and bayonetted anything that moved. Some militia fought, others turned their muskets upside down as a sign of surrender but their pleas for mercy were ignored and they died where they stood. For the redcoats the battle was now in their favour, closing on the enemy with their bayonets was everything they were

9

trained for, more than anything, the militia had a fear of redcoat bayonets and this was a fight they didn't want.

The Light Company charge was effective, as they rolled up the left flank, the fleeing militia were running into their own men in the centre, the result was complete chaos and a collapse of resistance. Tom was pushing his men forward, he tried to hold back and take in the situation and saw a militia boy no older than 16 screaming, his arms were in the air, a Grenadier plunged his bayonet into the boy's chest, he died instantly.

As he turned a militia officer ran at Tom; the officer swung his sword down at Tom's head it was obvious he was a militia man, no professional soldier would make a first strike like that! Tom lifted his musket over his head easily parrying the blade and kicked the officer between the legs, as the officer leaned forward in agony Tom swung his musket butt hitting him around the head knocking him onto his back; he then turned his musket point first and pushed the bayonet deep into the man's chest.

As Tom looked down at the dead officer his eye caught a small pistol in the dead man's belt; for some reason in the heat of the battle he decided he wanted the pistol and leaned down taking it for himself; then he turned back to the men encouraging them forward. As each redcoat followed Tom they plunged a bayonet into the dead officer until his body was a bloody pulp. He should have been repulsed by this but after seeing so much death in one day he felt nothing, absolutely nothing.

There were few muskets shots now, just screams, those of the rampaging redcoats and those of the militia being hunted down and gutted as they tried to flee. Death was everywhere but this time it was men wearing blue and civilian coloured clothing that died not red.

The militia were running away towards the town of Cambridge, they abandoned their positions and more importantly their artillery pieces. British officers were shouting and hitting their men with the flats of their swords ordering them to take prisoners; prisoners were taken but they were mostly militia who were wounded and disabled. The battle was over and the soldiers of the Light Company were too exhausted to pursue the militia, they cheered and waved their muskets in the air, the battle of Bunker Hill had been won but at a terrible cost.

Tom walked back down the hill of slaughter through the dead bodies, smoke and stench of a battle fought. Sergeant Major Riordan lay dead face first in a heap. Tom kneeled down beside the Sergeant Major and put his body out straight leaving the tricorn hat and his beloved sword on his chest. Tom made the sign of the cross and started to pray. Tom noticed Sergeant Major Riordan's pocket watch hanging out of his tunic, he checked the time it was 5 o'clock. He thought, "My god, I never believed so many men could die in 3 hours".

That evening sitting in the militia positions Tom and those few men in the Light Company who were not dead or maimed ate their meagre field rations around a fire; they were exhausted in their minds and their bodies, no one spoke. Tom's once fine uniform was in shreds and covered in mud and gore, he was bandaged around his wounded shoulder and his once white breeches were splattered with his own and others blood. He felt suffocated and opened his kerchief to breathe, he felt a small crucifix he wore around his neck; the one thing he had with him from his home in Tipperary; now was as good a time as any to pray; as he prayed he thought of his home and family in Ireland, they had never felt so far away.

Major Kellet using a musket as a crutch came and joined them; as men stood up he waved them down, "it's been a hard day men I know, but the regiment and I are so proud of you".

He motioned at Tom to come and ushered him away to speak.

"Well Sullivan, you are promoted to Sergeant and well done to you. I saw how well you fought this day and led the men charging the militia positions; also the Yankee officer you bayoneted was a general, Joseph Warren. So, there you have it promoted to Sergeant for bravery, leadership and we need you, too many officers and Sergeants died this day".

"Thankyou sir" Tom stood ramrod to attention as Major Kellet hobbled away.

"Sir, why did we attack the militia positions like that"?

Major Kellet stopped and turned back.

"Arrogance Sullivan, pure arrogance. Our generals never thought the militia would stand; well now we know they can fight and they want to fight as well. This is no longer a small local dispute in Boston and Massachusetts, we have a shooting war on our hands", as Major Kellet said this his head dropped, for one moment he looked broken then he made his way off.

Tom watched the medical orderlies and their carts picking up the wounded and carrying bloodied and broken redcoats back to the transports. He sat down with his men and took the pistol he had taken from the militia officer out and looked at it, it might come in useful one day; he put it away. This beautiful land why would anyone want to fight a war in it? It was then his mind wandered back to how his journey to Boston had begun.

Chapter 1
The Recruitment, Fethard, Tipperary 1771

There was nothing there, nothing; Tom Sullivan looked up and down the main street of Fethard, how many days now had he sat on a wall outside Nugent's Ale House thinking the same thoughts. Tom searched eagerly with his eyes for anything that would break the monotony of life in his home town.

Fethard, Tom loved it and he hated it both in equal measure. The people in Fethard all looked the same to Tom, thin; as was Tom. Living on a diet of bread, porridge and vegetables; eating meat was a rare thing, as were fat people, a rarity! For Tom it was simple, the Irish Catholics were thin and the fat ones were the landed gentry with their grand houses and land, they were what was known as the Anglo Irish but for Tom they sounded like they were English plain and simple; it was the way of things in Fethard.

The traders ambled past Tom pulling their horse and carts ready for the Fethard market day, there were the buildings dark, dank and plain boring, there was the river Clashawley and of course the old town wall, how many times had the old men regaled Tom with stories of how those walls still bore the marks of Cromwell's cannon balls. Fethard was full of history all right but none of it belonged to Tom. The old men were always there, sitting together in the Main Street when it wasn't freezing cold; smoking their pipes, talking about the town and how it was when they were young, Tom Sullivan was 17 years old and a young man with a real fear, would this be his life sitting in the main street as an old man making the same conversation?

It was a thought that made him tremble; in his young life the only foreign place he had been to was the nearby town of Cashel a few leagues up the road. Tom's father worked as a labourer on the estate of the local Fethard landowner, the Everard family, they had been in

Fethard for years, they didn't treat Tom's family bad but they had they the power in Tipperary and every Irish Catholic knew it, that's why you lifted your cap when you saw them if you wanted to hold on to the pathetic living they allowed you. Tom worked on their estate as well when he was needed, the few shillings he was paid for days of work was a pittance all right but as well as his native Irish he had learned to speak their English tongue as well. Hunting was something the Everards did a lot of and truth be told Tom enjoyed working on them, it gave him a chance to roam free around the fields and he had the chance to use a musket, he was a good shot and had bagged many a fowl for his masters. This was just a distraction, deep down Tom was frustrated with everything around him because he was where he was because of his religion and his surname and for those 2 reasons his life and his future would be one of poverty.

Tom knew what poverty was, he was living it. Cooped up in a labourers cottage with his father, 2 brothers and one sister, his mother had longed since passed away coughing herself to death in misery. Tom had been in the Everard mansion on their fine estate he could see what good living was and knew that his own home was not a cottage, it was a building that had a roof and a fireplace where the whole family ate and slept in one room, it was a hovel.

Tom looked up beyond the buildings in the main street and there was the mountain of Slievevenamon, the "mountain of the women", she was beautiful alright and Tom wondered how many people had looked at her over the years admiring her beauty, when mist sat on the top of the mountain the people would say she had her "veil on", yes Slievenamon was there and in Fethard, every day was the same and would always be the same and for young Tom Sullivan there was nothing there, nothing.

There was one thing that woke up Fethard every day, the English. Always at midday, a platoon of their redcoat soldiers would march though the main street led by an officer on a horse, they had a small barracks at Fethard and would do this so their officer would meet with the Fethard town Constable; to discuss things only they knew about and to remind the towns people who was in charge in Fethard. Their soldiers fascinated Tom, he never saw an English officer speak directly to any of the soldiers, he would only talk to a Sergeant, as for the soldiers they were a mixed bunch of English and Irishmen and even some from Scotland, now they were a funny lot, they had Irish sounding names and even sounded a bit like the Irish but they were different all the same. For Tom, the redcoats had two lives, marching in pace with their officers carrying their muskets and the other crawling through the Main Street of an evening after getting drunk in Nugent's.

Tom thought often about the English, "I don't like them and I don't hate them but they are what I need to leave this place". Just then a voice called out from behind him, "how are ye, Tom"? Tom looked around to see Joe Nugent standing in the doorway of his ale house. "Grand, Joe, grand" answered Tom. The whole town knew Joe Nugent, how could they not, he was a veteran of the French wars and had fought in the Kings army for many a year, he had a patch over his useless left eye, other scars of war on his face and he walked with a limp where he had taken a French musket ball in the right knee, not forgetting he was the proprietor of the best tavern in the Main Street, Joe Nugent was the reason Tom was sitting on the wall.

"You know Tom, if you want to talk to me, just do so, I've seen you everyday looking at the soldiers and I know what you are thinking, come inside and talk lad its too busy and I think you need to talk to me alone" said Joe in a fatherly manner. Tom said nothing and followed Joe inside the ale house, sitting down at one of the wooden tables Tom looked on the walls at the memorabilia from Joe's military career, old muskets, a cartridge box and bayonets hanging on the wall. "There you go again Tom, if you're not looking at soldiers marching then here you are gawking at my old cartridge box, spit it out lad, what's on your mind" asked Joe. Tom lifted up his head to compose himself he was nervous but excited, "Joe, I have to leave Fethard, I love me Da but I can't stay here, there must be more to see in my life than this town, I don't care for the English but I know if I become a redcoat then I have one chance to leave here, it worked for you Joe didn't it"?

Joe Nugent smile and lifted his head looking at the cartridge box on the wall, "Aye, Tom it did but as you can see I paid a heavy price lad", looking at Tom he lifted the patch on his left eye showing Tom a pitted lump of flesh over his eyeball, Tom grimaced at first and then looked back at Joe.

"That's right Tom look hard, this is war and if you wear the redcoat this is what you'll see and worse, my eye, the scars on my face, my crippled leg these are all wounds fighting for the English against the French at Minden, its over 10 years ago and I remember every moment, every volley, every charge, and the damn musket and cannon that gave me these wounds".

Tom thought for a moment then asked, "but Joe would you do it again given half a chance"? Joe laughed, "I would Tom, I know what you were thinking sitting out on the main street, I did the same myself 20 years ago, I took the redcoat and I was in places I never thought I would see, all you see here in this tavern is because of it".

"Were you fighting for the King Joe, for the English"? Tom asked, "Was I shite! I fought wearing the redcoat but I was fighting to survive, I had enough of being hungry, enough of poverty I had nothing here, so I fought and I killed for myself, for the men standing in the ranks beside me, for the colours of the 39th Regiment of Foot, so I could make something for myself, so I wouldn't end up sitting out there in the Main Street like those old men talking about how Fethard was 40 years ago, that's why I wore the redcoat Tom and I don't regret it one bit. There are dead Irishmen who lie sleeping in fields in Flanders and all over Europe, they wore the recoat for the same reason, they had no choice but to do little else. Remember another thing Tom, the men who will stand beside you in the ranks will be English, Irish, Scots, Welsh but they're like you, they have nothing in this world but the will to escape hunger and poverty. I made my own history Tom, stop listening to me and the other old men, you must make your own history or you'll go half mad here, you know this yourself lad".

Tom wanted to hear these words, before he could talk Joe butted in," I know your mind is made up Tom; just remember, the minute you walk away with the redcoats, prepare yourself it'll be brutal, there'll be floggings and days you wished you were dead, but you're like me when I was your age, you have no one to help you but yourself; you need to get yourself to the main garrison in Cashel you'll find the recruiting Sergeant there, so take the King's Shilling and I wish you god fortune, fight hard and use your brain you might even be back her in 10 years with enough coin to buy your own ale house, now you best be gone I have a tavern to run"!

Tom was a fit young man, he had to be, his village , Killerk, was a healthy distance from Fethard so he walked and ran everywhere unless he was lucky to get a ride on the back of a farmers cart. This day he had to walk, he had the one pair of shoes and they were falling to pieces, and as he walked he thought about how his father had made them for him out of bits of cloth and leather he had managed to grab together, "poor Da", he was the kindest man on this earth thought Tom " damn the English, damn the Everards and all your power, I damn well hate you for all you do to us, but I will use you and I will leave this place" without realising he was walking harder and faster, by the time he got back to the cottage he was panting and his feet were aching.

Tom looked at the cottage in the village, Killerk wasn't really a village just a few labourers cottages that were close to each other, there were his brothers and little sister playing outside as they always did, smoke from the ever burning turf fire was coming out of the makeshift chimney, the fields and hills behind were beautiful all right, horses belonging to the landowner would graze in them, if only things were different, Tom would never leave, but they weren't. "Tom, Tom where have you have been"? his little sister Margaret ran up to him and jumped into his arms only 8 years old Tom adored her. " I was only in town Maggie having a chat with Joe Nugent, now go off and play I need to speak to Da", Tom hugged her and let her down, she started running back to Toms brothers as soon as her feet hit the ground. Joseph, James and dear little Margaret, 8 years old and a child who loved life and everyone around her whoever they were, how Tom wished he could have that mind again. As his siblings loved their father then they looked up to Tom as the oldest brother, he fought their battles with other children in the town, he brought them food when their father couldn't; he was leaving them as well, his heart started to ache, his brothers waved at Tom and carried on running after their sister, Tom lifted his hand in reply but didn't move it he just looked at them.

When Tom walked into the cottage it was his heart's turn to now start beating quickly, sitting on a pair of stools by the fireplace was his father and the village priest Father Ryan. "Da, Father, how are ye"? Tom managed to mumble. Both men were smiling, "We're grand Tom, Father Ryan and I were just talking about you, come in now and sit with us son" his father beckoning Tom with his arm to come closer. Tom hesitantly sat down near them, "yes, Da I was just in the town".

"ah we know that Tom" answered Father Ryan " and did you have a good conversation with Joe Nugent"?

Tom looked at both men but couldn't find words to speak.

Putting his hand on Tom's shoulder his father said "Tom don't be worried now son, we know what you're about and who could blame you", Tom tried to answer but his father put his hand up to stop him speaking, "it's alright son, just look around you, I've lived here all my life as did my mother and father before me, just look at my hands Tom how hard they work for so little in return, your dear mother is buried out there in the field, I couldn't even afford a headstone for her". At the mention of his mother Tom could feel his chin wobble and tears formed in his eyes, how much he loved her and how much he missed her, her dying was painful enough it was the misery of the death that made him angry, sad and bitter at the same time. Tom looked at his father's tired, worn face then his hands, they were calloused, massive and told a story of hard work, he had no pleasure in his life but his children. " Da, I would never lie to you, I was going to tell you when the time was right that's all" said Tom keenly.

"Well Tom, now's as good a time as any, were not angry with you just talk to us lad" said Father Ryan.

Father Ryan was the best, a good man, he gave mass to the village but he also did his best to help the poor people of which there were many and him no better off himself. Father Ryan had given Tom and other youths in the village a great gift, education. "They keep you down by keeping you ignorant Tom, I won't let that happen to you or any of the children in my flock" and so Tom was taught to read, write and pray in Latin and he could do the same in English. Education was Tom's problem, reading had opened his mind, Father Ryan may have been a poor shepherd himself but he was dedicated to his flock and everything he had he gave to them, among these things was a battered, worn copy of Jonathan Swift's "Gulliver's Travels". How Tom loved that book, he knew it was fantasy and maybe he didn't understand the true meaning of it but all that mattered to Tom was that Gulliver went to places far and different and that was all he wanted.

Tom's attention turned backed to Father Ryan, "Father, I can't stay here, I have to move on away from Fethard, from this village, I want to help my father, the children but I can't do it here, I'm off to join the Redcoats I could die with them or find my fortune but I won't know if I don't try, there it is, you can try to stop me but it'll make no difference my mind is set".

Father Ryan looked back at Tom, smiling he said " I always told you Tom you have an enquiring mind, and your sense is good, yes you must leave Fethard to find your way in this life, I'm only here to talk with your father and offer him some comfort and God's love; he lost your mother now he is losing you, we have no intention of stopping you, just remember where you come from and those you leave behind and we pray to god we will see back here one day, aye, take the redcoat there is nothing for you here but misery and hard work, god protect you in your travels". With that he stood up and walked out of the cottage patting Tom on the shoulder as he left, outside Tom could hear the squeals and giggles of his brothers and sister as Father Ryan went out; everybody liked him he was a good man.

Tom's father said nothing, he looked at Tom and opened his arms, with tears in his eyes Tom ran to him and they hugged. It was a miserable business alright but that's how life was in Fethard; miserable and hopeless.

Three days later Tom was sitting on the back of a farmers hay cart on the winding road to Cashel, a few meagre possessions wrapped in an old bundled blanket was all he had with him. The farewell had been painful, his father and the children hugged him and all seemed to wail with the same sound of sadness as they tried to stop him getting on the cart. Tom was sad alright but he had a feeling of relief as well, it was the first time he thought he was taking control of his own life.

"May god bless and keep you my son" his father told him holding Tom by his shoulders and looking directly into his eyes. "I will Da, and I promise you all I'll be back to take care of you all. " Joseph, James, Maggie pray for me now will you? " Tom asked the children; they promised as one that they would then little Maggie put a small cloth package in Tom's hand, "Daddy says you mustn't open til after you leave Tom", my god she was a lovely child. Tom pulled himself away and jumped on the cart it was now or never he thought to himself, " I'll write you soon" he said as he settled himself, they said nothing but just stared up at him, the cart pulled away, he waved as did they, they got smaller, Killerk got smaller, then it was gone. Tom opened the package, inside was the tiny crucifix his mother used to wear, he put it around his neck.

There was no need to wait for a recruiting Sergeant with his free tankards of ale and Kings Shilling, the King needed redcoats a plenty; there was talk of war in America and with the French again so he would go straight to the garrison in Cashel as Joe Nugent had told him. Tom spent the ride looking around at his native Tipperary, green sloping fields that were beautiful on the eye in rain and sun; would the land look so different when he left Ireland he thought to himself? As the cart turned the corner at the foot of a hill the Rock of Cashel came into view, it was the only castle Tom had ever seen but it was a formidable one, imposing, dark and intimidating it had seen more than enough blood shed over the years, Cromwell's army had murdered many an Irishman there. As the Farmer drove the cart into the main street in Cashel Tom couldn't help but notice how much busier it was than Fethard, there were always more people in the main street, traders doing business with each other, but that was no surprise it was a real garrison town and where there were lots of soldiers the town would always profit, the farmers, the taverns and of course the prostitutes, everyone made money from a garrison. The main street bustled with people as Tom jumped off the cart, "good luck to you son" said the farmer, Tom thanked him and walked down to the garrison main gates. The garrison stood out from the rest of the main street, a plain high brick wall separated it from Cashel with a gate way entrance, what was inside who knew, although you could see the roofs of the barrack blocks and a flag with the English Union Jack that flew above them.

Two sentries stood on guard outside the gates, as he walked towards them he didn't feel any excitement in becoming a soldier just a yearning to leave Fethard. Tom had watched the soldiers enough to know their uniform well. They were of course wearing their redcoats, Tom knew enough that they were the 39th Regiment of Foot, a regiment raised in Ireland so they had Green facings on their coats, black leather stocks around their necks that held the head up straight, under their tricorn hats, their hair was soaped and frizzled with flour to make it look white as the common soldier couldn't afford a wig, then the hair was pulled down to a tight solid pigtail behind the neck, white breeches and black leather leggings over their boots, they wore two whitened leather belts across their chest that carried their cartridge box and a bayonet over a foot long, last of all they carried the famous "Brown Bess" musket, the real killing tool of the redcoat.

As Tom got close one of the sentries said "your business" in an accent that was Irish but not from Tipperary. "I've come to join" said Tom, "then you're an eejit" he answered, both soldiers started laughing, he threw his head behind him "that way to the guardhouse, the Sergeant there will sort you out, god help you cos no other idiot will around here" they both started laughing again. Tom was through the gates, looking inside he thought it was a grim old place, he could see the barrack blocks now, tidy but very basic and several buildings that were not unlike the smart houses on a landowners estate, maybe these were for the officers, he could see soldiers standing in their platoons being drilled, others were busy carrying supplies across the main yard, it was a barracks he thought not a palace. What was obviously an officer dressed in a fine tunic and a white wig under his gold trimmed tricorn hat came out of a side room and walked towards Tom, "Sir, I've", the officer walked past Tom without looking at him or turning his head.

Whack! A hand hit him across the face, Tom reeled back holding his hand over his now bleeding nose, a barrel chested Sergeant squared up to him, " come to join have you, well here's your first lesson; don't you ever address an officer again, have you got that you thick farmer boy"? He was definitely not from Tipperary, an English soldier from top to toe!

"Yes Sir" Tom answered,

"Yes Sergeant will do; cos that's what I am, now if you still want to do this follow me". Still shaking Tom followed the brutish Sergeant along the cobble towards the guardhouse, he turned back to look once more down the Main Street of Cashel, young Tom Sullivan walked through the door and away from his life as a boy in Fethard.

6 weeks Later – Training Barracks, Dublin Castle

"Make ready, present, fire"! The whole platoon fired at once the straw men they were aiming at were shredded by the 20 musket balls flying into them. "Recover" bawled Sergeant Riordan.

"Not bad boys, now, Sullivan get out here lad", Tom broke ranks and ran out to Sergeant Riordan stopping in front of him and standing bolt upright to attention. "Load up Sullivan and await my command to fire at the straw man in the middle". Tom nervously followed his drills, right foot moving behind, withdrawing a paper cartridge from his cartouche with his right hand, biting the top of the cartridge he kept the musket ball in his mouth pouring powder into the pan of the musket and gently easing the frizzen back over it to stop the powder falling out, with the remaining powder he emptied it down the barrel, spitting the musket ball down after it with the cartridge paper to keep it jammed in, removing the ramrod he shoved the contents to the bottom of the barrel then then brought the musket to the port position. "45 seconds Sullivan, too slow lad, the next time we face up against the Frenchies we need to fire 4 shots a minute, think about that boys he shouted out to the whole platoon". The lads were listening to Sergeant Riordan but it was obvious they were more interested in watching what would happen next with Tom. " Now, as I said before Sullivan the straw man in the middle, make ready, present," Tom took aim, now was the time, if he felt different being a redcoat, holding a musket was the most natural thing in the world for him "fire" Tom pulled the trigger, the hammer hit the striking plate igniting the powder in the pan, Tom didn't look away even though he could feel the right side of his face burn with the fire of the igniting powder, he felt the musket lift and then kick as the fire from the pan fizzed through the tiny hole from the pan igniting the powder that propelled the ball out of the barrel of the musket. The musket ball whooshed and shattered the head of the straw man, Tom stayed in the firing position. The whole platoon broke into a spontaneous "Hurrah". A slight smile came to Riordan's face, "steady in the ranks there, recover"! Tom brought the musket to the port position.

"Well you can certainly shoot Sullivan, I'll give you that, still a lump of an eejit but you can shoot", Tom laughed, so did all the other lads, even the Sergeant; "So now Sullivan, I think that it's the Light Company for you, fall back in the ranks". Tom fell back in with the platoon, his head was raised, chest out he felt proud. Moments like this were few and far between for a redcoat in training but for all the hardship Tom was not unhappy in his new life.

Sergeant Riordan then turned to address the platoon "Platoon attention, now lads listen up, Keep this weapon clean, a farmer has tools, a plough, shovels, a hoe, yours is a Brown Bess, look after it well and it will look after you, mark my words when your weapon is oiled, clean, your flint is sharp it will be the difference between you managing to get one more volley off against the Frenchies when their muskets are useless. Why do you think we beat them at Minden? Simple lads, superior musketry, we are the best in the world there's no army can go muzzle to muzzle with us redcoats and win, so we keep practising until loading your musket and platoon firing becomes second nature, have you got me lads?"

"Yes Sergeant", the platoon answered as one.

"Good, dismissed". Sergeant Riordan was like all the other non-commissioned officers in the regiment, they and all the officers of any length of service had fought under the colours in the Great War in Europe and all had tales to tell about the victory at Minden, it must have been a proud day for the regiment. Their officer was a Major Kellet, he was an Englishman and the very best type of officer; firm but fair and led by example at all times. However, how the major was made no difference; Tom learned from the brute of a Sergeant in Cashel that a private soldier would never address an officer directly.

Tom Sullivan was now a private in the "Almanza" training platoon of the 39th Regiment of Foot of His Majesty King George's Army. Almanza was a battle that the 39th Foot had fought and distinguished itself in as the Sergeants and Officers would always remind them.

Over the following weeks Tom changed, he prayed every day for his family but outside of this he rarely thought of them or Fethard for that matter. There was a set routine of endless drilling, uniform care, cleaning muskets and other equipment, Tom forgot everything of his old life, his uniform became less cumbersome to wear, he enjoyed marching and firing in rank, he loved bayonet practise, how many times had he killed the straw man with his sword bayonet. There were bad days too, he had been kicked and punched for dropping his musket on parade and for the first time in his life; he watched one recruit being flogged 20 strokes with a birch rod for stealing from the quartermaster store, they were all forced to watch lest they committed the same crime, it was bloody, it was horrible. But this was the life of a recoat he reasoned and he knew two things; he would be fed three square meals a day and wherever in the world the regiment went he would go with them. There was also Dublin, it was the first time he had been in a big city, rich men with their fancy ladies strolling arm in arm past their fine houses, large statues in the street and boats passing down the River Liffey, if Dublin was like this how did London or Paris look? This was his new life and this was his new family the 39th Regiment of Foot.

The platoon had its characters but they were mostly the same, young men from the country who joined the army to escape a life of hard labour and little reward. Among them was Campbell, big, loud and unlike the rest was from a city, Belfast, he was tough and an obvious felon and he let the other lads know it. Tom knew his type and waited to see when Campbell would show himself as the tough man in the platoon, he didn't have to wait long.

The platoon were always cleaning, uniforms, the barracks, equipment but most important of all their muskets.

Cleaning muskets would always be done as a platoon so they could be inspected by Sergeant Riordan after they were finished. On one particular afternoon the platoon were busily engaged in this duty in their barrack block. Campbell, as well as being loud was bone idle and standing up with his musket walked over to another recruit, Cullen, a young lad from Cork, who was busy cleaning his own weapon. Campbell threw his musket on the floor in front of Cullen, " Clean it Cullen and bring it back to me when you're done " he ordered. " Clean it yourself Campbell" answered Cullen. Campbell dragged him up by the scruff of his tunic and slammed Cullen against the wall, swearing into his ear. The whole platoon stopped their cleaning and looked up at the pair of them. "Now listen to me my little farmer friend from the country, you do as you're told, as always, by your betters or I'll beat the life out of you "he growled at Cullen in his strong Belfast accent. Before Cullen could answer it was Campbell's turn to be grabbed by the scruff of his tunic, picked up and thrown on to the barrack room floor! Dazed and confused Campbell muttered " what the Hell ". Tom walked over to Campbell and standing over him said, " Whatever you learned where you were dragged up in the whorehouses of Belfast, keep it there, we're all in this together, Catholic, Protestant there are no papists or whatever in this platoon no-one cares a damn, now clean your own musket ". Campbell made to get up slowly, as he did so he slammed his right fist into Tom's stomach doubling him over following up with a punch to the chin that sent Tom backwards landing on his arse. Campbell stood up, "whose next "? He shouted to the platoon. To Campbell's surprise, Tom didn't stay on the floor he was up on his feet, hurt but ready. "I didn't want this Campbell but here I am "he gasped trying to get his breath back as he put his fists and body into a pugilist's stance. Campbell laughed, "come on then Sullivan, the boy from Tipperary; let's see what you're made off "mimicking Tom's accent. By now every musket was dropped as the platoon gathered round the two men. Campbell advanced forward swinging haymakers, Tom didn't want to get hit again, Campbell was too strong, he ducked and slipped each   punch and the more Campbell missed the more frustrated he became. Campbell swore and abused Tom trying to provoke him but he wouldn't react. Campbell swung again, missed, splat ! Tom caught him with a perfect punch on the nose, Campbell staggered backwards, eyes watered, hand to his nose with blood trickling through his fingers. Campbell looked at the blood on his hand, " you Papist bastard ", he ran at Tom throwing another punch, too simple, Tom stood aside and punched Campbell in the side of the head sending him running head first into a wall landing in a heap. Campbell got up, dazed and hurt, he came back at Tom staggering forward; this time Tom walked towards Campbell, feinting a punch causing Campbell to lean back Tom kicked him straight between the legs, the whole platoon laughed and cheered, the kick to the genitals was more than Campbell could bear, such agony, he couldn't scream he grunted, groaned and fell to the floor holding his organs in both hands.

Tom knelt down over Campbell, "you know Campbell the lads in this platoon can't stand you, forget where you came from you half-wit bastard, it's because you're a bully and a coward, you only fight with those you think you can beat, this time you lost, we could kick you to death now all of us but we haven't, so be thankful and change your ways."

Campbell stared back at Tom, "Sullivan, I swear to god I will kill you if it's the last thing I do". Just then Sergeant Riordan walked into the barrack room bellowing," What's going on, why are you not cleaning your muskets, Campbell what happened to you"?

"Nothing Sergeant, Campbell fell over" answered Tom.

Riordan stared at both men, "damn right he did now get back to your duties, all of you I want those muskets cleaner than a nun's habit".

The platoon snapped back to work including Campbell and Sullivan, they continued to glare at each other Tom knew he had an enemy for life.

For part of their training the Almanza platoon marched out from their barracks in Dublin with the rest of the regiment to perform field manoeuvres in the countryside. It was a sight to behold; 800 redcoats marching through the county of Dublin with their officers on horses and all the supporting supply wagons needed to sustain a regiment in the field. For the men it was a relief to get out of the barracks but marching to the Wicklow mountains with a Brown Bess musket and full marching order was a challenge; by the time they pitched their tents near a village called Hollywood their backs were aching and their feet were blistered and bleeding after a long march.

Field manoeuvres were about training the regiment on how to operate when on campaign. Once settled, the men were schooled in light infantry work, skirmishing in broken order, scouting ahead of a main force, learning to tap load a musket, building defensive earthworks, the intricate manoeuvre of marching as a regiment from line into a square formation to defend against cavalry attack, even catching and skinning rabbits before cooking them but these were all country lads and living off the land was second nature to them. Tom loved every bit of it; even menial tasks like setting tents in a straight line. It was during this task that field manoeuvres turned sour for Tom.

The men were gathered around Sergeant Riordan who, while explaining the virtues of an ordered field camp, somehow managed to stray into another story of his part in the battle of Minden. Campbell had kept to himself since the barrack room brawl but raised his arm interrupting the Sergeant.

"Yes, lads if we weren't organised at Minden we would have lost, now what is it Campbell"?

"Sergeant, I have a terrible stomach cramp I need to use the latrine this minute", pleaded Campbell.

"Hurry up Campbell and come back quick you fat idiot, maybe the runs might thin you down a bit", ordered Riordan, the men laughed loud as Campbell ran off holding his stomach.

Redcoats were taught to stack their muskets standing up with the bayonets locked around each other; this allowed soldiers to grab them quickly if they came under attack. After setting their tent lines for the umpteenth time the platoon was dismissed by Sergeant Riordan and given 10 minutes rest before parading for their next duty. As Tom walked back to collect his musket he noticed 3 muskets lying in a heap on the ground, how did that happen? The men with him picked up their muskets but Tom's was missing. He started to panic, "where is my musket, has anyone seen it", he searched for it himself but it was nowhere to be seen.

The minutes of rest finished as quickly as it started, "all of you on parade now", bawled Sergeant Riordan.

"Oh Jesus, I'm in trouble now"! He was panicking with good reason.

The Almanza Platoon lined up, all with their muskets, except for Tom Sullivan. Sergeant Riordan walked up and down the platoon of soldiers and stopped when he got to Tom.

"Where is your musket Sullivan"? Sergeant Riordan was fuming.

"I don't know Sergeant, I left it stacked when we pitched tents when I got back it was gone".

Sergeant Riordan addressed the platoon, "Right, when I give the order to dismiss you will pair off and search this camp until we find this weapon, dismissed"!

The camp was turned upside down, tents were pulled over, even the quartermaster wagons were emptied and then there was a shout, "Sergeant, over here".

Tom and all looked to where the shout came from as a soldier walked back from behind the Colonels tent with a broken musket in his hands the butt of the weapon had been snapped off.

"Is that it Sullivan, you break the musket yourself and instead of owning up to it you try to hide it, the cheek of it behind the Colonel's tent"? Sergeant Riordan asked.

"Sergeant, I did not break my musket nor did I hide it", answered Tom.

"Then who did"?

As Tom searched for an answer he caught one person looking at him and smiling, Campbell, he should have known from the start! There was no answer to give; Campbell was paying him back.

"You will report to the Colonel this evening after messing, this will cost you pay for a new musket and no doubt you'll be flogged, now get out of my sight"!

The next day on morning parade the whole regiment assembled in a square formation. In the hollow of the square was a shirtless Tom Sullivan; his wrists were bound with leather to crossed halberds. The charge and punishment was read out by Sergeant Riordan, 15 strokes of a birch rod.

The Colonel of the 39th Foot, Colonel McBride sat astride his horse beside Major Kellet; he nodded at Sergeant Riordan and then turned to address the regiment.

"Men, when you serve in my regiment I expect your discipline, honesty and care of your arms to be beyond reproach. This soldier not only damaged his musket, he also chose to conceal his heavy handedness in a dishonourable manner, Drum Sergeant do your duty".

The Drum Sergeant went forward to Tom and offered him a piece of leather to bite on, Tom shook his head. The Sergeant leaned in close," take it you eejit, by the 10th stroke you'll bite your own tongue off".

Tom took the wise counsel and opened his mouth biting on the leather. The Drum Sergeant laid the first stroke on Tom's back; the leather was good it stopped him from screaming with each stroke being counted by a single drum beat. The pain was like nothing he could describe; he wanted to cry. Even through the pain he could see the disappointed faces of Major Kellet and Sergeant Riordan, his heart sank; Tom still respected them both.

By the final stroke Toms back was a bloody mess and he almost collapsed with the pain but in his mind he would not give Campbell the satisfaction of crumpling in front of him. The punishment was complete and a bucket of water was thrown over his back as the Drum Sergeant cut his wrists free. The shock of the water made him arch his back in agony.

The Colonel rode over to Tom, "You have been flogged for your indiscipline Private Sullivan but it is sure you are a brave man, take this", throwing a Shilling at Tom.

Tom stood to attention, "thankyou my lord".

The parade was dismissed; Private Cullen and others ran to Tom to support him. Campbell approached as well but with no good intent.

"Well done Sullivan, very brave, this should help you to look after your musket in future", he laughed.

Tom lifted his head and glared at Campbell," Campbell, if this makes you think we are even, so be it, but I warn you now; if you come near me again I won't just kick you in the bollocks I'll gut you like a stuck pig".

Campbell like any bully was uncomfortable at any form of defiance and scared of anyone that could better him, his face flushed red, he said nothing and walked away.

Three days later the march back to Dublin was an agonising experience for Tom; his feet ached as before but not as much as his back, the damaged musket had cost him pay and a thrashing but he had learned a lesson for life, trust no one but himself!

For the rest of their time in Dublin, Tom and Campbell kept their distance from each other but the first fight in the barrack room had its consequences, Campbell had obviously met his match but felt revenged and left the other recruits alone. In the meantime the wounds on Tom's back healed and training for the Almanza platoon continued unabated, drilling, marching, musketry, bayonet practice, care of uniform, they became one, marching as one. From their first fumbling volleys they all learned to fire 4 musket shots a minute, the mark of a true redcoat.

After 10 weeks they had completed their gruelling training and were ready to pass out. The platoon stood as one on the parade square. Behind them the rest of the regiment stood to attention with the colours of the 39th Regiment of Foot to the fore.

Colonel McBride addressed the men with Major Kellet and Sergeant Riordan standing beside him.

"Men, when you arrived here you were for the most part farm labourers, some of you had other trades. Now you are all the same, Soldiers of Private Rank wearing the uniform of His Majesty the King in his Army. More importantly, you are now able to wear the colours of the 39th Regiment of Foot, look at the Green facings on your tunics, this shows the regiment is raised in Ireland and we are known as the "Green Linnets". Believe me, I know you all, I will follow your progress and when I see you earn the single stripe of a chosen man or you rise to Corporal or Sergeant there shall be no man more proud of you than I. Yours is a proud history men, remember it well, when next you march into battle to the colours and the bravery of the men who carried them before you. Ours was the first regiment to deploy to India, the 39th fought at the great victory of Plassey, it has never disgraced itself in battle, Almanza, Fontenoy, Minden, more engagements where the blood of you forebears is remembered in glory to this day. I know you will continue their proud tradition. You are the Green Linnets, be proud of your history, your comrades in arms, a proud legacy is on your side and destiny will follow. "

At this; the colours were raised the Fifes and Drums played the General Salute and the regiment presented arms as a whole. Then Tom Sullivan and the men of the Almanza training platoon turned to the right and marched out as one to the tune of Lillie Bolero, ready to make history for the regiment and their own lives.

Chapter 2
The Sortie, Gibraltar
27th November, 1781

They came in the night, 2,500 men, almost half the Gibraltar garrison lined up in companies ready to go. The Spanish siege works had edged too close to the British positions defending the "Rock" and this night they would be destroyed. Leading the column was the Governor of Gibraltar himself, Lieutenant-General George Augustus Elliott, riding beside him was his second in command, General Ross; this was a major action by the British army garrison defending Gibraltar and it would be a night to remember.

Gibraltar, how could a strip of land a mile long have such strategic importance? For the Spanish it was a national insult; how could a European power with an overseas empire allow a piece of its own territory to be occupied by a foreign invader? For the French; Gibraltar gave Britain an opportunity to open and close a gate for ships entering the Mediterranean and an unequal naval influence that threatened their interests in the region. Britain's war in America was going badly and for Spain and France now was a chance to lance a very annoying boil; putting Gibraltar under siege they would eject Britain from the "Rock" once and for all. Governor Elliot had other ideas.

The 39th Regiment of Foot were part of the Centre Column under Lieutenant Colonel Dachenhausen, Grenadiers and Light Infantry, 3 Officers and 60 Ranks each. Dachenhausen, a grim faced German, and a veteran of the American War he was no fop and knew his trade well.

Sergeant Tom Sullivan of the Light Company looked his platoon of men up and down. Now 10 years a soldier and another veteran of the American Wars this was a different kind of action this evening.

"Now boys, no loud orders tonight, let's get those bayonets fixed and gently does it, I don't want any shot in those barrels for now, this is real killing work this night, don't think don't hesitate, put that bayonet into every Spaniard you see until I tell you to stop, have you got me boys"? Heads nodded back in response.

They were a mixed bunch, some were young Irish lads; others like Murtagh, O'Connell, Duggan were good men who had served with him in America, experienced soldiers and killers they had shared many hardships. So this night out they went, after 2 years of limited action and constant bombardment and siege this was their chance to put the fear of god into their Spanish foes. Each soldier carried 36 rounds of ammunition, no officers carried swords, no marching into battle with drums and fifes the whole operation would be around surprise.

" Right, on me now" as Tom turned he waved his arm, the Light Company filed out behind him with the rest of the centre column, marching through the British advanced positions they formed position in between the Left and Right columns and it was a formidable sight; 2,500 Redcoats in a line, ready to march into battle. Behind the attacking troops were companies of Royal Engineers carrying pick axes, shovels and other tools ready to do their own work. The magnificent Rock of Gibraltar in all its splendour loomed large over the raiding force how many battles had it witnessed over the centuries?

The officers in front signalled and the whole column moved forward, ahead of them they could see the fires from the Spanish positions only several hundred yards away, as they column crept closer they could even hear Spanish voices talking and the noise of musical instruments playing, that would soon be interrupted in the most violent manner. As the creeping mass of men and muskets neared the Spanish line Tom could hear himself praying, the same prayer he always made when he went in to battle, " Holy father, if I forget you this night, I beg thee not forget me".

40 yards to go still, no movement from the Spanish lines, the surprise was complete. The officers turned and waved their arms the whole column halted and as they had trained the 2,500 muskets were then loaded, no ramrods this night, powder and ball was dropped down each barrel and tap loaded by banging the stock on the ground.

Muskets loaded the column moved forward again within 20 yards of the forward trenches, there were shouts in the darkness; two figures could be made out running back to the Spanish lines, two bangs and flashes of light they had fired their muskets to warn their comrades, there was noise, shouting, movement.

Colonel Dachenhausen moved back to the side of the column and nodded at Tom. "prepare your firelocks", this was it the fight was on.

"Present", the front two ranks of the whole raiding party aimed their muskets at the Spanish lines,

"Fire", 1200 muskets fired a massive volley into the Spanish lines. There was a massive whoosh of noise and blinding fire among the line, none of the soldiers could see the effect of their volley but could hear the muskets balls smashing into anything they met.

Then along the column the order came out from several voices, "Charge, Charge, Charge"! There was no stopping the redcoats, they charged as one muskets levelled with bayonets to the front, screaming "huzzah" as they ran forward.

The charging redcoats could see the terrified panic in the faces of the Spanish soldiers, standing up in confusion after the mass volley, trying to pick up muskets and load them in a hurry, before they knew it the raiding party was on top of them.

The centre column hit the San Carlos battery, the charging redcoats still screamed as one, to the Spanish soldiers it was too much surprise, too much terror, some fired their muskets off with a ragged volley that brought down one or two redcoats, then they climbed out of their trenches and ran back to their main lines. For the unfortunate ones who stayed in the trenches they had no chance, the redcoats leaned down and bayoneted them where they stood, their resistance was short lived, those still alive dropped their muskets and raised their hands in the air screaming for mercy.

"They're on the run boys keep at them" shouted Tom. The Light Company charged over the trenches staying on the heels off the running Spanish troops.

Amidst the melee Tom noticed Governor Elliot on his horse beside General Ross observing the action on the left, out of the corner of his eye he noticed a Spanish Officer running up behind the Governor sword at the ready, time stood still as Tom ran to intercept him. The Spanish Officer raised up his sword to strike, Tom shouted "My Lord", Governor Elliot turned as did the horse under him, the flank hitting the Spaniard and knocking him off his feet, it gave Tom the time he needed as the Spaniard got up Tom drove his bayonet into his stomach. Governor Elliot observed the whole scene as a redundant bystander as Tom withdrew his bayonet and the wounded officer lay stricken on the ground beside his horse.

It was all ending now, the Spanish had given up their feeble resistance and up and down the siege works were running away to their second lines throwing away their muskets and anything that would weigh them down.

There was dead and there was dying, Tom could never reconcile killing; bearing this in his mind despite having done it many times before. Minutes earlier he was stabbing his bayonet into his enemies, now he was pouring water from his canteen into the mouth of the Spanish officer dying from Tom's bayonet stab to the stomach, as Tom cradled the poor unfortunate in his arms the soldier looked up at him muttering words in his own language. This wasn't Spanish though, he recognised the words, "Mother, Father, I see you, it's me Michael", oh Jesus he was speaking Irish. Tom answered him in Irish, "Yes Michael I see you too its Daddy, all is grand now son". Tom could feel the tension leave Michael's body, he seemed to relax, he smiled and then closed his eyes as his spirit went to the next world and not for the first time Tom could feel the life force leave the body of another wasted young man's life. Tom looked at the facings on Michael's tunic and saw he was in the Irish Legion of the Spanish Army. Marvellous Tom, he thought to himself, I come a thousand miles to kill another Irishman in a war that has nothing to do with either of us except escaping hunger and poverty. Tom laid Michael down making a sign of the cross on his head, he stood up composed himself and became Sergeant Sullivan again.

Good job too, Governor Elliot and General Ross were standing beside him. Tom stood bolted to attention, "Sergeant, I believe I am in your debt, your name" asked Governor Elliot.

"Sergeant Sullivan, Light Company, 39th Foot my Lord".

"Well met and good work with the bayonet Sergeant, I thank you again, best you attend to your duties"

"My lord", Tom saluted and ran back to his platoon. The lads had done their work alright and had come back now searching through the Spanish trenches for anything worth taking.

Watching Tom run back to his men, Governor Elliot turned to General Ross, "everything in life happens for a good reason, find out more for me about this Sergeant Sullivan".

Tom got his men back in shape, "Right lads, gather up their muskets, cartouches, ammunition it all comes back to the Rock with us tonight, you lot take guard of the prisoners while the engineers break things up".

The Spanish prisoners sat on the ground huddled together then they were stood up at bayonet point and marched back towards the Rock.

Colonel Dachenhausen walked back to the centre company after an officers gathering with Governor Elliot. "Sergeant Sullivan" he barked.

"Sir" answered Tom

"Once the engineers have finished their work, The left and right companies will march back to the Rock, followed by the centre company, I want your Light Company fanned across the rear to distract any Spanish sorties, questions?

"None Sir"

"Good, then deploy your men now I will deploy the Grenadier Company behind you in case the Spaniards come at us with anything stronger than a harrying attack, to your duties gentlemen."

The engineers had set about their work with gusto; fortifications were broken up with axes, shovels and any tools to hand. What was once an impressive set of Spanish trenches and siege lines were now broken piles of wood, bricks and mud not to mention spiked artillery pieces. Every Spanish musket, bayonet, cartridge box, anything that was thrown away or taken from prisoners was to be brought back to Gibraltar. The three companies that made up the sortie started to form up, the engineers piled their tools in wagons their work done.

As ordered the Light Company formed up in skirmish order to the rear of the raiding party as they formed up to march back to the Rock. Tom looked closely towards the Spanish reserve line, it was dark and difficult to make out but there was movement.

The Light Company waited never taking their eyes off the Spanish Reserve Line. "Sergeant look, to the left" shouted one private, all eyes turned and out of the darkness Spanish cavalry appeared; first several horses and riders and within a minute a whole squadron formed, a shout from their line and they drew their sabres and started advancing at the trot.

"Stand to men, prepare your muskets, kneeling position, do not fire until you hear my command", Tom barked at his company, 60 men went about their business in the way they had been drilled how many times.

"They look like heavy cavalry Sergeant, shall I order the Grenadiers forward"? Colonel Dachenhausen appeared at Tom's shoulder.

"No sir, my men are able" answered Tom.

"Very well Sergeant, let's see if Spanish cavalry are better than their infantry, carry on".

The Spanish cavalry advanced in line, from a trot they moved to the charge and came at the Light Company at full force, it was always a magnificent albeit an intimidating sight to see cavalry formed up and charging.

Tom looked at the faces of the Light Company, they were nervous alright but looking to Tom for orders.

"Right boys, remember we're the Green Linnets, let's show them how we stand firm, make ready" he shouted the familiar order. As 60 muskets went through the first drill for volley fire the relief was obvious for the men.

The Spanish Cavalry got faster and closer at full charge, the ground was thundering, sabres in the attack position, the troopers screaming at the top of their voices.

"Present", the Light Company muskets went into the aim position. This was about who could hold their nerve, if the volley was controlled they could stop the charge in its tracks; if it was rushed the Spanish cavalry would run through and trample the Light Company like corn.

Tom knew the fire discipline of the Light Company was without doubt, he had trained them for how many hours, he knew their nerve would hold.

The Spanish cavalry were almost on them then came the command the lads were waiting for.

"Fire"!

The volley was a wall of flame, smoke and the rhythmed crack of the Light Company muskets going off almost at the same time. For many of the Spanish troopers this would be their last sensation on this earth.

A storm of hot flying lead hit them with an immediate effect, men screamed in agony, horses whinnied as they fell forward throwing their riders, what was seconds before a majestic spectacle was now a scene of turmoil, the charge ground to a halt. There were many casualties, dead and wounded men and horses lying where they fell, those that weren't hit turned their horses, picking up wounded comrades where they could and raced back towards their own lines.

"Recover" bawled Tom and the Light Company brought their muskets back up from the firing position.

"Well done the Light Company"! Shouted Colonel Dachenhausen.

The lads lifted their tricorn hats waving them and shouting hurrah, redcoat fire discipline had proved itself again.

The company was busy cheering but one Spanish cavalryman stopped his horse in the retreat and turned back towards the Light Company, he was an officer, he stopped his mount then saluted with his sword and advanced at a trot and again broke in to a charge but completely alone, some of the redcoats were waving at him hoping he would turn around, this was honour but it was foolhardy.

Some muskets lifted up, "Leave him lads he's mine" ordered Tom.

Tom walked directly in front of the line of redcoats as if showing himself to the charging Spanish officer, who obliged and turned his horse towards Tom.

As he raised his musket and aimed it, the process was as natural as if he was still shooting fowl in Tipperary.

The Spanish officer dug his spurs into his mount, leaned forward in his saddle and pointed his sabre straight ahead charging directly towards Tom, this was now a one on one duel, the cavalry officer against the light infantry Sergeant, who would prevail?

Closer and with speed the heaving mass of horse muscle and pointed steel got closer to Tom, officers, privates all stood still to look at the bizarre spectacle; 25 yards to go when would Sergeant Sullivan fire?

Tom squeezed on the trigger of his Brown Bess, he didn't look away even though he could feel the right side of his face burn with the fire of the igniting powder, he felt the musket lift and then kick as the fire from the pan fizzed through the tiny hole from the pan igniting the powder that propelled the ball out of the barrel of the musket. The musket ball whooshed, if it didn't hit the cavalry man then Tom one would be run over and slashed to death in an instant.

"Thud", the noise of the musket ball hitting the Spanish cavalry officer in the chest, knocking him backwards and throwing him off the saddle of his horse landing in a heap. The horse came to a stop and ran back to be with his master.

"Huzzah" shouted the Light Company, another reason to wave their tricorns in the air.

Tom walked forward and stood over the dead cavalry officer, "rest in peace my friend" then he helped himself to the Cavalry sabre and taking the horses reins walked with it back to his men, who gathered around him still cheering.

Unbeknown to Tom, there was another spectator to the duel, "that man Sullivan again, he has nerves of steel" Governor Elliot said to General Ross, "well ,our work is done, now let us get our men back to the Rock, make much noise, fifes, drums in full marching order, I want our enemies to see us now

The companies reformed, Sergeants shouting orders, colours unfurled. Governor Elliot now wanted to let the Spaniards know the British Army were there and were taking their time.

As the raiding party marched back to the British advanced lines the Spanish siege works were burning, shells were going off, it was a spectacle alright.

Within 30 minutes the Light Company were back in their barrack room in Gibraltar, Tom looked at the lads, they were jubilant and fired up and why shouldn't they be? They had dared and they had won. Tom had been in the army now for 10 years and had felt this way many times, he had tasted victory and also defeat in equal measure. It was always at times like these his mind would wander back to Bunker Hill, "My god, if that was a victory what was a defeat"? A question Tom asked himself many times since that terrible day, "a thousand casualties to take a hill that was abandoned a few days after, for what purpose"? As soon as he started thinking this way he realised grinding his teeth wouldn't change history or bring back the good men who fell beside him, he cast the thought aside and went back to watching his men.

The men were cleaning their muskets and kit. Duggan said "you know that was the Utonia Regiment back there, they're Irish".

"I know" answered Tom "so what".

"So there it is Tom, we Irish kill each other easily, if we could learn to kill the English the same, maybe Ireland could be free"?

"Maybe we can go back home and teach them all how one day, maybe we could get the Yankees to teach them too, they were certainly good at killing us in America, maybe this is a silly damn conversation Willie Duggan that could get us both strung up for treason if an ambitious Englishman heard us", Tom's voice was low but direct, staring directly at Duggan who now wished he hadn't brought the subject up.

" Aye, you're right about the Yankees, they did know how to kill us, a good Sergeant always has his feet on the ground, just you keep us alive" answered Duggan.

"That I will with you and the other lads Willie by concentrating on killing the Spaniards and Frenchies, now go and get the men sorted and get some grog down you, the governor has given us all liberty this night, as for Ireland, we can liberate her another time"!

Duggan nodded got up and walked out, a stupid conversation but one Tom had in his mind a thousand times. He reconciled himself that all that mattered was the here and now, what was in front of him, survive the day the night, the liberty of Ireland from the English would come another day.

The fact was Tom Sullivan enjoyed the life of a soldier, all of it, maybe he didn't consciously know it, but he did. Each day had an order and a variation at the same time, especially on campaign.

The day he left Ireland he knew he would never see it again, his father, his brothers and sister, he missed them, he prayed for them but he knew he would never set eyes on them again.

Tom never thought of himself as a future Tom Nugent with a wooden leg and his own ale house back in Fethard. He was amazed he had survived the American War, a gruelling campaign and so many lives lost and for what purpose? As for Tom, he had fought all over the colony and suffered only a few minor wound, how could that be?

He always thought there was an enemy musket ball destined to finish him one day so he went into battle cautious but without fear, if anything he cared more for his men than for himself, when he lost a man it cut him to the bone; it was this thought that kept him going.

That evening in the Governor's Building, General Ross gave his report to the assembled officers, "we have hurt them militarily gentlemen, more importantly we have scared them, they have no appetite for fighting us on the ground in column or by direct assault, we have bought ourselves time while they think on their next course of action".

Governor Elliot nodded in agreement, "thank you General Ross, we certainly gave them a bloody nose tonight, ensure you commend all your men, they fought well this night".

"However, I fear our respite will be short and soon our old enemies the French will arrive, so enjoy this evening but our work carries on in the morning, you are dismissed gentlemen".

As the different officers filed out of the meeting room Major Kellet of the 39th approached Governor Elliot, "My lord I understand you wanted to know more about one of my men, Sergeant Sullivan of the Light Company".

"That I do Major Kellet, your Sergeant Sullivan bayoneted a Spanish officer who was about to fillet me during the sortie, then I watched him down a Spanish Cavalry Officer, carry on".

"Yes my lord, I had heard, he enlisted to the colours in 71 in Ireland, Garrison duty in Dublin and London then America. He served under me in all of the major engagements there, Bunker Hill, New York, Brandywine and with distinction. Mentioned in despatches on a number of occasions, wounded slightly several times but still survived the most brutal engagements. He is a natural leader, respectful but not cowed by senior ranks, one of my most experienced non-commissioned officers and has all the makings of a future Regimental Sergeant Major".

"Thank you Major Kellet, I may have work for this Sergeant Sullivan" you may carry on. A busy man, Governor Elliot, he returned to study his plans.

The atmosphere in Gibraltar Town in those early hours was jubilant, the town was lit up, all the taverns were open, the locals, soldiers everyone was out and why not, just when the Spanish thought they were getting close to the Rock a major sortie had broken their efforts. Governor Elliot had rewarded his men the opportunity to get happily drunk and drunk they would be. Sergeant Tom Sullivan wanted a drink but he had a woman and he wanted to see her as well.

Lara
The women in Gibraltar were beautiful, tanned and naturally sensual. Tom had liked the women back home and the Yankee women in the American Colonies but these were different and one woman stood out amongst them all. Lara, she was a rare beauty alright.

Lara was always waiting for him, beautiful, sullen, rebellious, naughty, and vivacious. Lara had the beauty and personality that would make the richest women in London and Boston spit with jealously, how did Tom know? He had met them and had some of them as well, Tom was no pretty boy but women liked him, there it was. But Lara wasn't rich; she was a young woman of Gibraltar and every man who saw her wanted her, but Lara had eyes for one man only and that was Tom. "Hello my Thomas "she would say to him and he loved that, he loved her accent.

Lara was the owner of the Soldier's tavern in the main street, it had been left to her by her late father; her mother had died when she was a child. The Tavern was the soldiers favourite drinking hole and why not? Lara had every beautiful girl in Gibraltar with ample bosoms working there, a feast for a drunken soldier's eye!

One night working in the tavern, Tom had pulled a drunken Corporal off Lara and sent him flying out of the door with a boot in his arse. Between Tom's looks, his Irish accent and his defence of her, the attraction was immediate. Lara was a Mediterranean woman in a hot climate, unlike the miseries of the British Isles; Sex was something to be enjoyed not just a religious or child producing duty. That first night Lara gave herself to Tom after the tavern was closed. Their love making was passionate, rough, exciting and their bodies were joined completely and she was his. Tom loved Lara alright but she was not the first woman he had been with. For Lara it was different, Tom was now the man of her life and it would always be so.

As Tom walked through the door of the tavern the atmosphere was lively, packed full of drunken redcoats, singing songs, pouring ale down their throats and celebrating victory; they deserved it. Lara was in the middle of it, his eyes met with hers; she was pouring ales into tankards, she smiled and winked at him, every time Tom laid eyes on her he thought her more beautiful. It was then he noticed a group of soldiers in the corner, not drunk and keeping to themselves, the uniforms were too fresh; reinforcements had come in on a supply ship a few days previous; that was probably some of them. A Sergeant stood amongst them, very much in charge. The Sergeant looked around the tavern as he put his tankard to his lips, he looked past Tom then back at him, there was recognition and he walked straight up to Tom.

"Well, well, Tom Sullivan, a long way from Dublin and a Sergeant now, has your back healed yet"?

Tom recognised the harsh, ugly voice immediately and the face apart from more brawling marks hadn't changed much either.

"Campbell, why are you here, and now you're a Sergeant as well, I thought the regiment would have made better use of your talents"? Tom answered smiling.

"Oh yes Sullivan, how's that"?

"Oh you know, Garrison duty in that shit hole you come from, Belfast, beating defenceless whores, helping the sheriff to evict poor Catholics from their cottages, real man's work. But you know it's different here Campbell, here people fight back they're called real enemies".

Campbell's faced reddened, "I thought the Yankees would have killed in you in the colonies, still it gives me the chance to break your face in Sullivan".

"Really Campbell the last time you tried, I remember I kicked you so hard in the bollocks they came out of your nostrils".

The whole Tavern burst out laughing, loud and long

Campbell stood up fuming, just like the barrack room in Dublin.

"Campbell, I don't hate anyone as a rule but in your case I can make an exception because deep down you're a coward, a bully, a whoremaster, everything I like about a real good coward and yourself in particular, fat and pig fucking ugly".

The other soldiers were laughing so much they were dropping their tankards of ale,

Campbell was so angry he was hyper ventilating, his eyes were bulging, he walked towards Tom, arms by his sides, fists clenched,

Tom stayed calm, "well Campbell are we going again, no stealing muskets, no floggings just you and me", the whole Tavern anticipated a fight

The tavern door burst open a Colour Sergeant walked in wearing full battle order, "up and out all of you and back to your posts, the Spaniards are forming up we need the garrison to stand to, now" he shouted.

Tankards were guzzled down, cross belts and tricorns were picked up and the tavern emptied out of soldiers.

Campbell walked out with his men, "next time Sullivan you're all mine", he growled.

Tom said nothing.

It was just him and Lara now, she sat on his lap and hugged him, for a few moments they could forget the siege and be lovers together.

"I've got 10 minutes Lara" said Tom as he took off his cross belts.

"That's enough time my Thomas", Lara smiled as she locked the door of the tavern and they moved into the back room of the tavern where Lara slept, then they made love.

Lying in his arms afterwards Lara suddenly sat up, "I'm scared of that man my Thomas, who is he"?

"Someone, I knew a long time ago, he was and will always be one thing, a bully, but don't ever be scared of a bully that's what they rely on to get their way, leave him to me, now I have to go darling unless you want me confined to barracks", Tom smiled and winked at Lara as he stood up and got dressed.

"I'm not scared of anything my Thomas as long as you are with me. I love you with all my heart my Irishman, when this madness is over take me with you; I have no fear of anything as long as you are beside me. "

Tom leaned down and kissed her, "let me finish this madness first Lara, then who knows where we will be". Tom picked up his cross belts and musket and walked out.

Lara watched him leave; she knew in her heart this Campbell Character was bad for her and Tom.

As Tom walked back to the barracks he mused over the nights happenings. He had led a company of soldiers in the first major engagement between the British and Spanish forces in two years of siege; had saved the life of the commander of British forces on the Rock, taken the lives of two men by his own hand within minutes of each other, met with an arch enemy whom he never thought to see again and still had time to be with his woman. Tom believed in god, fate, destiny, whatever it was called and knew that everything in life happened for a reason. After surviving the war in America and seeing so many of his fellow soldiers die beside him he felt he was only alive because he was a good soldier and because god had directed the musket balls that would have killed him into his leg and shoulder not his head or chest.

Tom knew all of the night's events were part of a chain and would affect him and Lara one way or another, how? He would find out soon enough.

Chapter 3
The French Arrive, May, 1782

The atmosphere was tense at the headquarters in Algeciras of Vice-Admiral Antonio de Barcelo commander of the Spanish siege army. Unlike other military commanders of the day, Barcelo was not born into a rich family but had come up through the ranks with years of experience fighting the feared pirates of North Africa. The same could not be said of the two men with him; The Duc de Crillon and the Chevalier D'Arcon albeit they were both experienced soldiers and came from the nobility of France.

Barcelo slammed his hand down hard on the table, knocking over the wine glasses that spilt onto the maps showing the Spanish and British siege positions.

"As I have told you Monsieur Le Duc, I, my officers and indeed my soldiers have done everything possible thus far to subdue the British garrison, my fleet has the Rock under blockade the British cannot receive any supplies, eventually they must capitulate. They have 5,000 soldiers not to mention civilians crammed into a piece of land a mile long, they cannot leave by land or sea, patience and time Monsieur le Duc that is my advice, the victory will be hours." Barcelo finished speaking, he was exasperated and perspiring, who were these two Frenchmen to come and tell him how to take the Rock?

The Duc de Crillon waited then chose his words carefully, all of them intended to sting Barcelo, "My, my admiral you talk of patience and here you are knocking over wine glasses."

Barcelo bit his lip, he had said enough already.

"Well, let me come to the point, Paris and indeed Madrid are impatient with your lack of progress, you speak sense with regarding to starving the British out but the fact is we do not have the time for this. You are aware that the British war in their American colonies has gone disastrously for them. A war both our kings support; it might be that even now the British are treating with their former subjects for peace".

"You can understand then; that if Spain is to regain Gibraltar as part of its sovereign territory once more and if both our countries are to have control of the Mediterranean then it must be done now. The British have 40,000 soldiers and a fleet of over 40 ships committed to the American War; I wonder what would happen to your precious land and sea blockade when these soldiers and ships are sent back to Europe?"

Barcelo was about to answer.

"Hold your peace admiral, I'm not done", this time De Crillon slammed the table.

"You tell me you have done everything, all I can see is a naval blockade and siege works, where are the attacks? Thus far, it seems the British have taken the initiative, how could you allow 2,500 redcoats to sneak out of the Rock and destroy your forward positions without any warning, are you not ashamed of this admiral?"

Barcelo stiffened at this remark and de Crillon realised he had gone too far. "Forgive me admiral, I know you lost many good men that night, I am as frustrated as you by the situation and my words reflect this inappropriately. I have faced the British many times; I was at Minden when their damned redcoat volley fire destroyed our cavalry, I know how formidable they can be."

"However, as I informed you earlier, King Carlos has appointed me overall commander of both Spanish and French forces in this operation, we have discussed a plan of action in Paris, the Chevalier D'Arcon will now explain it."

Chevalier D'Arcon walked forward to the wine covered map," Messieurs can we address the map if you please", a smile on his face as we wiped some of the excess wine away with a napkin.

"I think we have debated the situation enough, a land attack across a small strip of land on its own will allow the redcoats to concentrate their musket and artillery fire, our troops will be massacred for no gain. By sea, yes we can blockade the British but do little else."

"What is required is a simultaneous attack by land and sea that hits them at their weakest points. To this end, you will see ten

47

massive floating hulks arrive here in the next few days, these hulks are designed to be floating artillery batteries, along with some of the best engineers in France they have been constructed to carry as many guns as possible and will be so heavily armoured with additional planking they will be unsinkable."

"I have already inspected the British positions and the Kings Bastion will be their target, our floating batteries will sail into position on mass; bombard and destroy the British fortifications there and once this breach has been made assault troops on landing craft will pour through and into the Rock itself."

"At the same time, we will bombard them from our land siege positions, once we compromise their defences at the Kings Bastion we will mount a land attack through the causeway, the British will be stretched to breaking point. You have questions, Messieurs?"

"I understand and I to my own surprise I am in agreement with your plan, Chevalier D'Arcon, when is this to happen" asked Barcelo.

"A good question Admiral, the hulks are only partially complete, we have much work to do on them, you have I believe, 28,000 soldiers under your command, more troops are on their way from France already, this will be our grand attack!

" In the meantime, I want the English land defences softened up, I want concentrated and regular fire on the British Willis's Batteries up on the Rock; they must be neutralised otherwise they will slaughter our troops and stop the land attack in its tracks."

D'Arcon looked to Barcelo and de Crillon, "that messieurs is the plan in its most basic form now let us attend to it in detail".

The three commanders of the Franco-Spanish army then returned to inspect the proposed troop deployments on the wine splattered map.

Willis' Artillery Batteries – The Rock

The Rock of Gibraltar was a gift for a military commander defending a position, for the attacking commander it was a nightmare. A small causeway linked the Rock to the Spanish mainland and the British had positioned some of their best artillery in the rock as it towered over the land crossing. A mix of high elevation and natural and engineered cover had given their guns an ability to create a killing field that the Spanish dared not cross. For the British they had the confidence that they were in the main; safe from the guns in the Spanish siege lines. Collectively, these sets of batteries were known as Willis'. It was a virtually impregnable position.

For an infantry soldier in the siege; besides being on watch on the land and sea defences for endless hours, much time was spent hauling supplies from the main supply depot in the town to the forward defence positions facing the Spanish siege lines.

In the case of Willis' the Royal Engineers had carved out a series of tunnels in the Rock that allowed men and supplies to walk to the various artillery batteries without breaking cover.

The Princess Ann's battery was an artillery officers dream, sited inside the Rock at the end of a tunnel, with its barrel pointing out of a man made aperture; it could hit the Spanish forward positions at will while hiding behind its own breastworks and the natural cover above, below and beside it.

This particular morning Tom's platoon were engaged carrying ordnance to the Princess Ann's battery.

This was hard physical work manhandling carts full of gunpowder and cannon balls through and down dimly lit tunnels sculpted out of the Rock. By the time the men had dragged the carts to the battery and unloaded them at the magazine they were exhausted.

"Well done lads, sit now and rest up, get some water down you for 10 minutes" Tom told the men, they didn't need to be told twice as they slumped down where they stood.

Tom knew the artillery Sergeant, a man called Mason and walked up to him, "well, there's your ordnance Sergeant Mason, how are the Spanish this morning"?

Mason was busy siting an artillery piece but recognised the voice and turned around.

"Ah Sullivan, look for yourself out the front, they've been trying hard to hit us but their cannonballs are bouncing off the rock either side of us" he laughed.

Sure enough, looking out past the barrel of the gun, the view was impressive, Tom could see all the Spanish forward positions; as their guns fired he could see the fireball, the smoke and then watch the cannonballs as they flew upwards and bounced harmlessly off the Rock.

"Well, I'm envious of you Sergeant Mason, safe and snug up here, maybe I should join the artillery"?

Both men laughed, "I wouldn't bother Sullivan too noisy".

Tom smiled and turned to walk back to his men, looking out from the battery one last time, Tom saw the flash, the smoke and then heard the report from a Spanish cannon. He then heard the loud constant whistling sound as the cannon ball flew towards Princess Ann's.

After 3 years of siege and 10 years a soldier Tom could tell by the noise of a cannon ball being shot how close it was and where it would hit.

Without thinking he turned and ran back to his men.

"Lads this is bad, get back now and get down, run" Tom shouted at his men. They needed no further encouragement they ran as one away further from the battery and dropped down hugging the ground.

"Bang", the cannon ball flew into the opening, smashed through the breast works of the battery, and then everything slowed down, dust, damage and gunners already dead.

"It's in the magazine" the last words that Gunnery Sergeant Mason uttered in his life.

"Bang, flash", everywhere was deafening noise, blinding light. Tom had managed to run back a good few yards but the blast blew him off his feet. He came to lying on his back with bits of wood and various debris covering him, there was smoke everywhere, then his hearing came back this is going to be bad he thought, he got up and walked back towards the battery, more like staggered.

"My platoon on me, 39th where are you"? he shouted through his dust coated throat. Sure enough, his men his men started to appear, dazed, confused, covered in dust but seemingly all alive.

Not so the gun crews, they were in a mess, bodies everywhere, gruesome, bloodied, twisted, Tom's lads were shocked and hesitant.

"Come on now lads, let's help them, move the dead aside we can look after them properly in a while, it's the wounded we need to help now".

As they began the gruesome process of working their way through the dead and dying Tom found Sergeant Mason, lying on his front on top of another gunner. Mason's back was in shreds and he was dead alright, but the man underneath him was still alive. Good for you Sergeant Mason, Tom thought to himself, he sacrificed himself to save one of his men; he remembered a prayer Father Ryan taught him as a child in Tipperary, "Greater love hath no man than this, that a man lay down his life for his friends". As many times before Tom prayed for Sergeant Mason as he tried to lie his body down with some dignity.

Sending one of his men off to get help Tom and his men began their grim work.

Governor Elliot soon got news of the catastrophe at Willis'. Before long he arrived with General Ross. As he viewed the scene around him, a surgeon and medical orderlies had arrived and there was some order to proceedings but it was still a butchers den.

"My poor boys" he said to himself shaking his head. Turning to an Royal Artillery Major he got back to business, "right, get the battery backup and firing right away, give the wounded as much help as we can, I want a full report on casualties and the condition of the battery by this evening".

As he turned to leave the Governor noticed Tom helping an orderly put a wounded gunner onto a stretcher. "Sullivan is that you"? he asked.

"Yes my lord" answered Tom attempting to stand.

"No Sullivan, stay as you are, look after that man, by your appearance I can see you were here when this happened".

"Yes I was my lord; fortunately I was further back when the magazine blew".

Nodding his head Governor Elliot commented," you certainly have the luck of a soldier Sullivan, you just stay alive don't you, well done anyway" at that he turned and walked away with General Ross.

He was right Tom Sullivan had survived again.

Governor Elliot turned to General Ross to speak to him about Tom Sullivan yet again. "Right, now I have work for this Sergeant Sullivan, this lucky soldier, inform Major Kellet that I want this Sergeant Sullivan in my office first thing in the morning.

The tavern was quiet that evening; 15 Gunners died at the Princess Ann's battery and it had affected morale badly. As ever, it was packed with soldiers but they were in a sombre mood, drinking but keeping to themselves, no singing this night. Lara knew the mood of the men and served their alc with a knowing smile and an occasional pat on the back. Lara felt different though; despite the loss of the men there was happiness inside her she couldn't explain. It wasn't just having Tom Sullivan in her life, she was singing all the time while working and her voice soothed the feelings of the men and she moved around the tavern. Suddenly a hand grabbed her wrist! Lara was startled and tried to pull her arm away. "Now, now missy no need to be unfriendly". It was Campbell, sitting with 3 other soldiers all of whom were laughing at Lara and obviously in thrall of their leader. Lara's happiness had turned to fright and embarrassment as she tried to get away from Campbell.

"Let go of me now you bastard before I smash this tankard over your head", motioning with her head to the tankard in her hand.

"Sullivan's girl getting angry now, give the tankard to me you dirty whore for a Tipperary bastard". As Lara become more distressed so more did Campbell and his minions laugh; she looked around the tavern at the other soldiers surely one of them would help?

Just then a voice said, "allow me", the tankard was jerked from Lara's hand and smashed over Campbell's head. Campbell went flat down on the table smashing his face; he stood up holding his head in agony, blood smeared around his nose.

"You again"!

"Yes Campbell, it's me the Tipperary bastard", Tom was not alone, Duggan, Murtagh and O'Connell stood beside him. As the words left Tom's mouth he struck Campbell with the tankard on the point of the chin knocking him flat on his back.

52

As the minions stood up terrified at the fate of their leader they tried to back out of the tavern.

Duggan asked," Sergeant, with your permission"?

"Carry on lads". The minions then disappeared under a flurry of punches from the 3 veterans of the 39th Foot.

Campbell, for the second time in his life was in a punch drunk daze. Tom picked him up by his lapels. "This time I will make the threats Campbell, if I see you near my woman or this place there will be no more kicks in the bollocks or tankards in the face, you will end up in the sea in pieces", he threw him back on the floor.

Campbell and what was left of his 3 minions were then picked up and thrown out of the tavern onto the street to the cheers of every soldier in the tavern.

The mood in the tavern was now rousing; soldiers were singing and raising their tankards to the lost Gunners and the 39th Foot. Tom and the 3 lads settled down for a drink it had been a hard day at Willis'. If Lara had ever been in love with Tom Sullivan before; she was dying for him now and took every opportunity to sit with him and let the world know he was her man. Tom pulled Lara close to him.

"This Campbell business won't finish here, I know him and he'll be back for more, of that I'm sure, here take this".

Tom produced a very small pistol from his knapsack and gave it to Lara. " I got this when I was in America, keep it loaded and primed at all times and close to hand, you may need it to protect yourself if I'm not around, do you know how to load it"?

Lara nodded, she stared at the pistol, it more than a weapon, for Lara it was a sign of Tom's love for her, she hugged and squeezed him for all her worth.

Days in Gibraltar started much the same, reveille; rouse the troops up, parade, inspection and duties for the day. One morning in September started differently for Tom Sullivan, Major Kellet took the morning parade as normal, once the soldiers of the Light Company had been dismissed to their duties he called Tom over.

"Sergeant Sullivan, you cheat death again, 15 gunners killed at Willis' and not a scratch on you, how do you do it?" a rhetorical question from Major Kellet.

"I think we faced too many cannonballs fighting the Yankees Sir, we both know a good shot and bad shot from an artillery piece".

"Aye, Sullivan, we faced a few out there, anyway it appears you are a man in demand, you are to report to the Governor's building, Governor Elliot requires your presence straight away" said Major Kellet with a thin smile.

"Indeed Sir, does that mean I'm in trouble or is it another matter", answered Tom.

Major Kellet laughed, "if you come back flogged then you were in trouble, otherwise I presume he has work for you, stop doing brave things and perhaps you'll be left alone, now be off with you".

Within 10 minutes Tom was waiting outside Governor Elliot's office.

"Sergeant Sullivan" shouted the Governor's Aide De Camp and in Tom marched standing bolt upright to attention in front of the Governor's desk.

Governor Elliot looked up from the papers he was reading.

"Sergeant Sullivan good morning, take your ease, we must speak at length as I have work for you. What we speak of in this office Sullivan must not be passed on to any living soul, do I make myself clear?

Remaining standing Tom relaxed his stance, "yes my Lord".

"You have served in his majesty's army long enough to understand that any commander of an army is only as good as the intelligence he has regarding his enemy. To be precise Sergeant, I had my informants in the Spanish Camp but they have now gone silent. I can only presume that they are discovered and hanged and this leaves me blind to the intentions of our Spanish and French foes. However, the last messages I received from my unfortunate spies was that the enemy are busy building what can only be described as "floating batteries", ships that are not made for the seas but will carry an immense amount of guns that will blast our sea fortifications in advance of a major attack on our positions, questions".

54

Tom thought for a moment "only my own observations my lord, we can all see how busy it has become behind the Spanish lines, there are more troops but also more civilians, hundreds if not thousands seem to be gathering in Algeciras we can see them there".

"Correct, but I cannot defend the Rock on scraps of intelligence and what we can see from our spyglasses, I must have more which is the very reason why you are here".

Tom braced up, "What will you have me do my lord?"

"Sullivan, I understand you speak their Spanish tongue and you also have an appearance that I'm hoping the Spaniards won't challenge. We need to know what they are doing with those hulks. Get over to the other side and bring me back everything you can. How many ships, guns, crew, what sails they have, whatever the detail it will be of use to me, I must know how we can damage those things before they can drop cannonballs on us at will."

"make your preparations to get across the Spanish lines, how you achieve that is your choice; but after our sortie the Spanish have doubled their sentries so a land crossing will be difficult. In any case, a diversion will be created that will keep the Spanish busy, just get me what I need, if we can't stop these so called floating batteries the Rock will be lost it's that simple."

"Remember Sullivan, if you are caught you will be hanged as a spy, in any case this is not a request it is an order. any questions?

"When do I leave my Lord"?

"The sooner the better, tomorrow evening at the latest, choose two of your own men to go with you and good luck".

"My lord" as Tom turned to leave, Governor Elliot had one final comment, "Sullivan, there is another reason I have chosen you, you just don't die make sure you luck continues,"

Tom smiled and walked out.

It had been a typical evening at the tavern, tankards full and singing and Willie Duggan had drunk a skin full of ale by the time he stumbled out to walk back to barracks. As Duggan walked half singing and mumbling a tune from his native County Kerry even in his drunken stupor he knew he was being followed.

"Who's there, show yourself you blackguards"! He challenged defiantly adopting a fighting stance. Before he could utter another word several men came out from the shadows behind him. A woollen blanket was pulled over his head and arms. Duggan arms were pinned under the blanket by one man while the others laid into him. Duggan was kicked and punched him until he was unconscious and collapsed in a heap on the cobbled street.

"Alright boys, thats enough to let Sullivan know we're still here, pull the blanket off him" ordered Campbell.

As the blanket came off him, Duggan was a bloodied and beaten man, his head and face horribly swollen, as soon as his attackers appeared so they disappeared.

The next day on parade Major Kellet was furious as he addressed the men of the 39th.

"Last night a man from the Light Company was set upon and beaten unconscious. Whilst this individual will recover from his injuries I cannot be more angry that we have lost a man to thuggery and not enemy action. Governor Elliot is aware of this incident and his instructions are clear. If there are any further incidents of this manner the culprits will be dealt with severely. The Provost Officer is investigating the manner, that is all. Sergeant Major dismiss the regiment to their duties".

As the men fell out, Campbell approached Tom, "I hope yer man gets better Sullivan", smirking as he said it.

Tom had punched Campbell how many times before but now he had to use all his discipline to keep his clenched fists by his sides.

Staring long and hard at Campbell he spoke firmly, "Your time will come Campbell, don't worry".

"What does that mean Sullivan", again whenever Tom confronted him Campbell wasn't his usual bullish self and seemed startled by Tom's words.

"You're a hard man alright, but you have no brains, your own thickness and stupidity will let you down in the end".

Before Campbell could answer Tom had walked away. The confrontation that had started all those years ago in a barrack room in Dublin would finish in Gibraltar; both men knew it.

That evening in the tavern Lara was subdued, sullen, and miserable. Tom didn't have much time so he pulled her out of the tavern to talk away from the noise and ale. "But where are you going my Thomas, when will you come back"?

"You know I can't tell you what I'm doing and when I'll be back, well, when you see me next, that's when".

Lara stood a full head under Tom and hugged him tight, her head buried into his chest. Tears ran down her cheeks, she knew he was doing something dangerous, while he was in Gibraltar, she knew he was safe but this was different, if he came to see her to say farewell he was going outside the Rock and this scared her.

Lara kept her head on Tom's chest, "I am carrying your child my Thomas" she whispered as tears ran down her face, not sad, she was smiling.

Tom felt his whole body shiver and he kissed the top of her head; so there is more to life than surviving each day by killing, this was life, this was a future. He pulled her away and put his hand on her stomach, Lara touched his hand, and they were both smiling.

Lara steadied herself, looked up at Tom and held his face in her hands, "my Thomas, just remember I love you and come back safe" then she kissed him.

He turned and picked up his musket and walked away down the street; Tom was thinking of Lara's words but his mind was already on the mission.

Lara watched him walk off, but unbeknown to her someone else was watching the scene. Tucked into an alleyway, Campbell laughed to himself. "Ahh, what a touching scene, a lover's farewell. Don't worry lassie, while that bastard Sullivan is away I'll look after you just fine!

Chapter 4
The Mission, August, 1782

Colonel Dachenhausen and Major Kellet were among the few men that were informed of the mission. Tom chose two men with swarthy appearances, Hogan and McGann, they changed out of their uniforms into the clothing of Gibraltarian townsfolk, they were armed with knives and an officer's pistol each, then they were then briefed on their part in the mission.

"So lads that it, it's down to us, you know where we are going, what we are really doing, I'll tell you over there on the Spanish side" pointing towards Algeciras.

"Questions"

Both men looked at each other," if we come back will the Governor reward us with something" asked Hogan.

"That he will Hogan, free ale and your own whore for the night"

They all laughed, what else could they do, this might be their last night on this earth.

The diversion the Governor mentioned was to be a massive artillery bombardment from the British Lines onto the Spanish land positions, along with a massing of infantry that would make the Spanish concentrate on receiving another sortie on their siege lines. In the meantime, Tom and his two men would be taken on a British Gunboat across the bay with the intention of making land by rowing boat just behind the main Spanish Camp at Point Mala from where they would make their way to Algeciras on foot.

In the warm September climate of the Mediterranean darkness came late; but by 9.30 in the evening the Spanish watched from their siege lines as companies of redcoats started to form behind the British forward trenches. Every British officer and private thought they were making another sortie on the Spanish and readied themselves for battle or so they thought. Fifteen minutes later every battery the Gibraltar garrison could muster opened up on the Spanish advanced lines and especially on Fort San Felipe; the nearest Spanish position to the sea from where "Europa", a British gunboat would try to sneak past.

The Europa pushed away from the British positions at the Old Mole just as the bombardment commenced.

The Europa was one of a dozen makeshift gunboats constructed at the orders of Governor Elliot with the aim of countering Spanish ships that had been preventing supply ships getting into the Rock. Gunboat was a mute expression; the Europa had one 24 pounder cannon and nothing else.

Standing on the deck of the Europa, Tom, Hogan and McGann could see the British batteries open up, the flash and fireball from each cannon and then the bang, within seconds they could hear the shouts from the Spanish lines, chaos, confusion, now was the time to get across the bay in their vessel.

Lieutenant Packwood of the Royal Navy and commander of the Europa approached the three men. "Gentlemen, my orders are to get you as close to shore as possible once we get past the main Spanish camp, after that I hope you have your rowing arms with you and good luck", Lieutenant Packwood laughed and walked away.

Slowly, the Europa moved through the water, the sea was calm, all seemed to be going well, then there was a lull in the barrage, this was not good.

The Europa drew level with Fort San Felipe, the captain, the crew, all on board the Europa were tense, staring intently at the fort, there was no noise just the squeaking of the gunboat's timbers, just a bit further and they would be past the forts guns and away.

Where was the British barrage, why had it stopped? Shouting, movement, activity it was obvious the Spanish lines were coming back to life after hunkering down under the bombardment.

Then from the fort, flashes of light, "down, down" screamed Lieutenant Packwood.

After the flashes came the bang of the fort's guns they had the Europa in their sights and every gun was trained on it.

As Tom and every man on board hugged the deck of the Europa cannon balls smashed through the timbers of the gunboat, large, sharp, horrible splinters of wood were flying everywhere, men were screaming, the deck was covered in broken wood, debris, smoke, there was nothing to do but wait for a break in the barrage. McGann got up in his knees to look around, a voice shouted "get down you fool" whoosh a cannon ball took his head clean off his shoulders, there were screams of horror as the headless torso spouted blood then fell forward, the furious firing started again, the Spanish had a British gunboat in their sights and within range and wouldn't let this opportunity go.

The Europa was a sitting duck, Lieutenant Packwood crawled over to Tom, "Sergeant, I can do nothing but try to get my ship back to the Rock, your rowing boat is on the other side of the ship, I can draw their fire while you get away, good luck!"

"Godspeed to you and your men Captain, Hogan follow me". Tom and Hogan crawled through, under and over broken wood and sails then crawled down the netting to a small rowing boat.

Too small to be noticed they used their oars to shove away from the Europa and leave her to her fate, still hearing the thuds of cannon balls hitting the gunboat they dared not to look back as they strained every sinew of their muscles to escape danger.

They pulled the oars for all their worth and slowly the Europa and the fireballs from Fort San Felipe became smaller and smaller. Now it was them and the water, the main Spanish camp at Point Mala came into view, how many flames from the soldier's campfires, it was massive.

"Look at those camp fires Hogan, there are 20,000 Spanish soldiers there waiting to get into the Rock and put us and everyone we know under the bayonet, now row hard and get past it, we start walking soon".

There was a relief from escaping the carnage on the Europa that gave them energy to row hard, before long the small rowing boat banked onto the beach in the darkness between the Spanish camp and Algeciras. As the boat pulled up both men jump onto the shingle to avoid getting wet and not give any sign of how they had arrived on the Spanish lines.

"Right Hogan, now I will tell you what we are here to do, as of this minute we avoid speaking any language but Spanish, from here we walk straight to the port where we should see a number of massive hulks being constructed. We need to find out everything we can on them, how thick is the wood on them, how many guns could each of them carry? That's just to start with, keep a vivid memory Hogan, no drawings, no notes; we have nothing on us that could give us away apart from acting foolish. Once the job is done we split up and make our way separately back to the Rock".

It was dark and before long the two men were walking on the road to Algeciras, it was a busy road, soldiers, traders, plain citizens of Spain, everyone was travelling up and down it; they soon blended in and for a brief moment felt a sense of freedom at being able to walk down a long road after 3 years of siege on the Rock, unnoticed by anyone and having a close up view of their enemies.

Algeciras was a hive of activity, there was almost a carnival atmosphere , soldiers everywhere of course, the taverns were heaving, traders of all sorts with stalls were set up not to mention no shortage of prostitutes.

The other presence was obvious, the French, they were everywhere. Soldiers in their hundreds mingling in with the locals, Tom recognised some of the regimental markings from his time fighting them in the American colonies; this meant the French army were there in strength. French soldiers were to be expected but there were a lot of sailors and what appeared to be engineers; this meant a French fleet was at Algeciras as well; the sooner they got to the port the better. It wasn't just the army and its hangers on that crowded the port city, there were people there in their thousands, rich and poor alike, Tom overheard the conversations they had come as spectators to watch the "grand attack".

It was late by this time; both men were tired and needed rest. "Well Hogan, there's no need to rush this, we find a room in a tavern if there's one free, we eat, drink very little and start fresh tomorrow, I will do the talking you just nod your head and say "si ", got it"?

"Si, Senor" answered Hogan

"Bueno, Vamanos", within half an hour they were sitting outside a tavern both enjoying a tankard of ale. The tavern was packed full of Spanish and French sailors all drunk; Tom and Hogan had never seen so many whores in their lives, they must have been shipped in from all over Spain and North Africa. Every drunken sailor had a woman sitting on his lap and Hogan was staring as if his eyes were ready to pop out of his head. "No time for that Hogan, we have work to do; we head for the port in the morning". At that they went upstairs to their room, as Hogan climbed exhausted into a cot; Tom lay on the floor across the door with his officer's pistol beside him, like Hogan he was tired and was asleep in moments.

The morning was a beautiful one in Algeciras, Tom looked up at the clear blue sky, the type one could only see in the Mediterranean, a far cry from the wind and rain of Tipperary he thought to himself. Both men went downstairs and the innkeeper served a meagre breakfast of bread, cheese and a mug of coffee but they enjoyed what they ate and wolfed the food and drink down.

Breakfast done they made their way to the quayside of the port; following the large groups of hungover sailors returning to ships and labourers come in from the countryside looking for work. There were no guards on the quayside; security was non-existent and they were able to walk wherever they wanted.

Then they came into view, there they were docked at the quayside, the so called "Floating Batteries", maybe eight or more and they were massive! Hogan looked at Tom aghast, mouth wide open; Tom shook his head in a "don't speak" manner. Up close the hulks were even bigger, so big he felt scared looking at them.

As a soldier Tom had travelled in ships of the Royal Navy many times, not to mention the perilous voyage across the Atlantic, they were fine, powerful ships , known as a "Men-o'-War", but these hulks were something different.

Governor Elliot's intelligence was correct; these vessels were not made for long sea voyages. What they were created for was attrition, the hulls were powerful, additional planking had been added to the gun side of each hulk for extra protection from cannonballs. Each ship had all its batteries on the one side so it was clear they were useless fighting at sea, they had the one purpose; to sail into position and fire on the sea defences of the Rock until it was smashed to smithereens!

Within minutes they had been hired for the day by a ganger to load supplies onto the hulks, now they could get a close look at them from outside and within.

Work started straight away, they saw some labourers picking up boxes of supplies and followed them up the gangplanks onto the nearest hulk, the "Pastora". Once inside the Pastora something became very clear. There was no open deck; the working operation of the hulk would be completely enclosed. Just walking around the hulk while it was in dock was unbearable with the heat, what would it be like with all its guns firing?

All day they worked under the hot Mediterranean sun, by the end of the day Tom and Hogan had seen inside each floating battery, all ten of them, counted the guns on each and even counted the sails to judge their manoeuvrability and sea worthiness. What they couldn't find out was a way for a cannonball to breach the protective planking on the battery side of each hulk.

Their days work done, each labourer was paid for their work in silver "Reals" that saw an exodus of men back to taverns of the port of Algeciras. The day had been good and both men had achieved what they set out to do but Tom Sullivan was an experienced soldier and was uncomfortable with success easy found; he pulled Hogan to one side.

"Listen up Hogan, we have everything we need, go back to the tavern and wait for me I want to have one more look at the quayside, when I get back we make our way to the Rock separately".

They parted company, Hogan to the tavern and Tom back to the quayside.

Within minutes Tom was back and he realised what they had missed. They had spent all day on the floating batteries and had ignored the rest of the portside; there were warships everywhere!

The British had always been well aware of the Spanish fleet but it was now combined with a French fleet. Tom made his way along the quayside counting over 40 ships, but the real surprise were transport barges maybe several hundred of them, he felt a panic grow inside him; a massive bombardment by the floating batteries and the combined fleet and then the landing of troops in the transport barges, how could the Rock stand against this?

He knew he had to get back to the Rock as soon as possible and get this information to Governor Elliot.

As he turned a rough hand pushed him hard in the chest, "Que faites vous ici monsieur"? it was a French Marine pointing his bayoneted musket at Tom.

Tom was startled and staggered backwards a couple of paces, that was when the Marine saw the handle of the officer's pistol in his belt. Both men knew what was to happen but Tom was ahead of the game; he grabbed the barrel of the musket and lifted it upwards pulling the Marine forward whose stomach fell onto a knife in Tom's hand.

As Tom pushed the knife in deeper he saw the life force leaving the Marine's face, but the man did his duty to the last and squeezed the trigger on his musket, "bang" off it went and on a quiet dockside the noise was deafening.

Tom killed when he had to, not because he wanted to; he dragged the marine behind some barrels and ran swiftly back to the tavern; already he could hear shouts and activity where he had killed the Marine.

Within minutes he was back in the tavern, as he walked through the door he saw a sight that that made a now difficult evening worse.

Hogan was drunk with a prostitute sitting on his lap; he was singing a song "the British Grenadiers". Tankards of ale were put down, French, Spanish they all looked around, the woman was thrown off   Hogan and he was grabbed by several of the gathering mob. All of the attention was focused on Hogan, he realised what he had done, he sobered up immediately and looked at Tom as he was being manhandled. Hogan jerked his head and eyes to one side in a "get out now" motion. There was nothing Tom could do, he backed himself out of the tavern and walked briskly towards the town.

Hogan would no doubt be interrogated and brutally so, Tom had to get to the Rock before Hogan gave him up which he eventually would. He reckoned he had several hours at the most not forgetting the dead marine at the quayside.

Decisions; did he try to find the boat or would this take too long and would he draw too much attention to himself? There was no other way to it; he would have to walk back through the main Spanish camp at Point Mala.

Within a couple of hours Tom was in the middle of the Spanish Army, it was dark by now; no pickets, no sentries, nothing! He walked straight in it was clear there was no expectation of an attack by any enemy and like Algeciras it was full of civilians. Tom walked straight through the camp and came out the other side dressed in the uniform of a Grenadier in the Napolese Regiment; borrowed from a drunken soldier asleep at the back of a tent.

Before he knew it Tom was standing at the back of the Spanish forward lines, he was that close to the Rock, just there across the causeway. How to get past the Spanish lines?

Just then his luck changed; the evening artillery battle between the Spanish and British forward lines commenced. The British batteries at Willi's opened up and the Spanish soldiers in the forward lines hunkered down hiding under the barrage. This was it, now or never.

He ran as fast as he could and jumped over the nearest trench pulling off the Spanish Grenadiers tunic and throwing it away. As the British barrage stopped he could hears shouts in Spanish behind him as he ran through the neutral ground. The next sound he knew well, flying musket balls, he was being shot at from the Spanish lines.

Tom ran as fast as he could, he was screaming at the top of his voice, "Sergeant Sullivan, 39th Foot"!

The next noise was musket balls flying at him from the British lines, still he ran, by now his lungs were fit to burst between running and screaming then he tripped and fell face down; his energy was spent he couldn't move any more, the firing stopped and he heard footsteps.

He looked up and saw several redcoats standing above him with bayonets pointing at his head.

A voice asked "who goes there"?

"Sergeant Sullivan, 39th Foot, I must see Governor Elliot at once" Tom panted.

"Really? 39th Foot dressed in Spanish breeches and boots, maybe you could see the king if you please"!

Before Tom could mutter an answer a musket butt hit him in the face and he was out cold.

"Wake up Sullivan" he heard the words again and again then felt something cold and refreshing on his face; it was a medical orderly bringing him to with a wet cloth.

As he woke up he saw he was in Governor Elliot's Command Post. The Governor was standing over him with General Ross, Colonel Dachenhausen and Major Kellet.

"Well done Sullivan you survived again, what of your two men"?

"The Spanish got them both my lord, one killed, the other captured".

"God bless them both, let us hope we haven't lost them in vain, make a report to Colonel Dachenhausen when we are done, so what do have for me Sullivan"?

"Your first intelligence is accurate my lord, there are floating batteries at least ten of them; they are formidable. The wood is thick by several feet; we must speak with our senior gunnery officer and devise a method of how to hurt them. I assure you our cannon balls will not penetrate their hulls, more likely they will bounce off them. As for guns, between them all the batteries have as many as 200, if they can bring them all to bear at the same time their firepower on a single position will be immense".

"So how will we sink them Sullivan, everything has a weakness"?

"Not in the normal way my lord, To our advantage my lord, these hulks are so large, they will come into place and probably will sit still, they cannot manoeuvre and will be a sitting target, we must find a week point and keep hitting it, if we can't hole them then we can set them on fire, if we use red hot shot and keep pounding them they must catch fire eventually."

Governor Elliot turned and looked out of the window of the room across the bay towards Algeciras, his worst fears confirmed.

"What else Sullivan"?

"The floating batteries are not the only challenge my lord, the French are there in strength along with the Spanish they must have around 40 ships of the line for their combined fleet. What I also counted were almost 300 troop transport barges".

Governor Elliot remained staring out the window, "go on Sullivan".

"Algeciras is full of soldiers Spanish and French; by my estimation if we count the numbers each barge can carry their numbers could be as many as 30,000 troops. The town is also full of civilians, I mean thousands of them, they are talking freely that they have come to watch the grand attack, it is as though half of Spain is coming to watch Gibraltar won back by the Spanish crown and they want to be there to witness it".

Governor Elliot turned back to look at Tom, "you have been there Sullivan, seen these hulks, their barges, the French, tell me what you think"?

"My lord, I also got through the main Spanish camp at Point Mala, it too is full of more men than would be normal; my belief is that the floating batteries will attack the Kings Bastion, it is the only logical place they can hit as there is no other point where they could land troops from the sea. If they can damage our batteries and fortifications enough they will use the barges to land their troops. At the same time as we are pressed at the Kings Bastion I have no doubt they will attack across the land causeway at the same time".

"Anything else Sullivan"?

"My lord, at Bunker Hill we marched against an enemy that fired on us from entrenched positions, we couldn't go any way but straight at them and they put sustained fire into us and we were slaughtered sure enough. This will be no different my lord, we reinforce the Kings Bastion and wait for them to sail into position and we keep hitting them with everything we have. To my humble eye as far as naval matters are concerned those hulks are finished and ready to sail, I spent my time loading supplies onto them so the attack will come to us soon".

"Very well Sullivan, I am in your debt again, you are dismissed". As Tom walked out Governor Elliot and the other officers went in to conference.

Back in Algeciras, the Duc de Crillon had been informed of the captured British spy, he had ordered the officer holding him to "extract" as much information as possible from the prisoner but he was to be kept alive. Several hours later the Duc was joined by Chevalier D'Arcon and Admiral Barcelo as they entered the guardhouse of the joint allied headquarters where the prisoner was detained. Entering a cell they could see that Hogan was a battered pulp, unconscious and close to death, he was barely standing held up by the ropes around his wrists. A French infantry captain stood beside Hogan along with two shirtless men; sweating after their brutal examination of Hogan.

"So what do we have"? The Duc asked as he held a handkerchief to his nose and mouth, the stench in the cell of human sweat and other activities was unbearable.

The Captain braced up, "Monsieur Le Duc, the prisoner has been stubborn; only now has he confessed to being an Irishman serving in the 39th Infantry regiment of the British Army. He has also told us that he was here to spy on the floating batteries".

"Well, well, how things come back to you, the 39th Foot, I remember your regiment at Minden how well they fought that day yes very stubborn, still, what a contradiction, here you are an Irishman fighting for the very people who enslave you, how is that possible"?

Despite the pain he was enduring Hogan lifted his head and tried to look at the Duc through his swollen eyes; surprised by the Frenchman's English and the words he said but did not answer.

The Duc continued," you are well aware that as an enemy soldier dressed as a civilian you are afforded no rights as a prisoner of war and so you will be hanged as a spy. However, if you have sense I have another way for you. Tell us more about your mission and indeed about the defences of Gibraltar, everything you know. I can see to it that you will receive attention to your injuries and then you can serve in an Irish regiment in the French or Spanish army, thus you will live and have the chance to hurt your hereditary enemies, the English, what do you say man"?

All in the cell waited for Hogan to answer; eventually Hogan breathed gasping for air and muttered through his bloody lips and broken teeth, "39th Foot that's my loyalty, English, French, Spanish, you're all the same, one king replaced by another, I will tell you no more".

Hogan dropped his head down as if passing out.

The Duc addressed the captain," So captain, as he pleases, interrogate him further for any information about the defences of Gibraltar, I do not care what he tells you; anything can be of value, I want a scribe in here to record his words, if he dies so be it, if he survives he is to be hanged as a spy".

The Captain and the two brutes nodded their understanding. As the commanders of the allied army left the stinking cell Hogan prayed repeating the "Our Father" and "Hail Mary" as the first punches hit his face and stomach.

It was late, Tom had made his report, all he wanted was a drink and to see Lara, he strode purposefully down the Main Street, too many emotions in his head, McGann and Hogan both gone, he prayed it was worth it.

Campbell had stayed away from the tavern since the last confrontation with Tom and Lara but had done this for a purpose; he wanted revenge on them both and this night he would have it!

Like a hunter stalking its prey, Campbell waited until the last drunk left the tavern; pushed out the door by Lara.

Lara busied herself picking up the many drinking vessels from the tables, she suddenly felt uneasy as though she was no longer alone.

It happened too fast, a strong red clothed arm went around her neck and pulled her backward off her feet, she screamed as she dropped the tankards onto the floor.

"Now missy, your lover boy is away, so I'm here to look after you tonight, no interruptions".

Campbell again, she recognised the voice and could see from the corner of her eye a sharp blade held close to her face.

He held her tight around the neck, Lara thought she would soon pass out and knew what would happen when she did.

Lara was gasping but defiant, "Tom said you were a coward and a rapist, now I know Campbell you bastard, you're no soldier just a coward"!

Campbell was hurt by the words and pushed her face down over a table starting to lift her skirt. He was growling," I'm as good a soldier as him and I'm no coward now shut your face whore"!

Campbell's hand pushed Lara's face harder on the table but she knew her words were working she struggled to speak.

"Don't compare yourself to him, you pathetic man, force yourself on me but I won't yield; you coward, you couldn't have a woman any other way could you"?

All the while she delayed Campbell; Lara knew she had one chance and reached down to a pocket in her skirt.

As she did so the door of the tavern opened inwards and Tom Sullivan stood there staring at them both; he was intense but calm, "Campbell, let her go"!

Campbell backed away his arm still around Lara's neck but this time the knife was pointed towards Tom, eyes full of hate.

"Sullivan, you have a habit of appearing always at the wrong time, but this time I'm glad you're here, you can see me slice your woman's face, then I'll kill you and rape her".

"Still, the coward Campbell; put her down and fight me like a man, just the two of us".

"No deal Sullivan, first I cut her up a bit, enjoy this", he was laughing he had Tom where he could hurt him. The blade pressed against Lara's throat.

Bang! Campbell screamed like a hyena, his eyes turned in his head, he dropped the knife, drawing blood on Lara's throat but not seriously injuring her, just like those years ago in the barracks in Dublin, Campbell was holding his genitals with both hands, but this time there was blood horrible amounts of it; he fell onto his back in agony. Tom looked at Lara she was holding the small pistol Tom had given her, it was smoking and he realised she had shot Campbell right where it hurt.

Lara's eyes were wide open, vacant; Tom pulled the smoking pistol from her hand and sat her down. He walked over to Campbell and stood over him, "well Campbell, no more raping defenceless women for you".

There was so much blood; Campbell was dying that was for sure.

"You couldn't leave it alone could you, god forgive you for your sins Campbell, I'll pray for you" said Tom.

"Damn you Sullivan" Campbell muttered.

"I'm already damned Campbell, but your more damned than me, now die with some peace in your heart, I don't hate you Campbell, god didn't create you this world did and I hate this world".

Campbell said nothing, his whole body arched then relaxed, teardrops fell from his eyes down his cheeks, he looked past Tom and breathed his last, he was gone.

Tom made the sign of the cross and turned back to Lara, holding her by her shoulders he looked directly at her, "Go back upstairs and clean yourself, cover the wound on your neck and do not come back down here until tomorrow morning. You say nothing; do not speak with anyone of what has happened here tonight, do you understand Lara"?

Lara nodded, she said nothing but tears were running down her face, she hugged Tom tight then turned and went away as he instructed her.

Campbell's body was found in an alley far from the tavern the next morning by a guard patrol. An investigation took place with the Provost Officer, Colonel Murray, concluding that in the absence of any witnesses, Campbell had probably been killed in a dispute. The only bone of contention was the murder weapon that was found close by, a small pistol, a type only found in the American colonies.

Colonel Murray was an experienced soldier; he too had served in America, he could dig deeper if he wanted to but he was a veteran in dealing with criminal matters in the British Army and had made enquiries about Campbell's character. "He's a bad un", that was the only answer he received. Yes, Sergeant Campbell was killed in a dispute unknown assailant. Colonel Murray looked at the American pistol and put it in his belt, "spoil of war"; he thought to himself and wrote up the report accordingly.

Chapter 5
The Grand Attack
September, 1782

The allied commanders meeting at Algeciras was a battle of wills, the Duc de Crillon was making the case to press the attack of the floating batteries for the next day, standing beside a detailed plan of the Rock and pointing with a walking cane at the area of the King's Bastion the Duc was in no mood to compromise. Around him and opposing his opinion stood the most experienced and capable military and naval commanders of France and Spain; his French colleagues, the Chevalier D'Arcon and the Prince of Nassau and the Spanish Admirals Barcelo and Bonaventura Moreno.

"Messieurs, I fully understand your concerns but you are all experienced in military matters, you well know that we will never have perfection in our preparations but the attack must happen as soon as possible".

The Duc was doing his level best to stay calm but was close to losing his temper; he was particularly annoyed that the Chevalier D'Arcon; the architect of the floating batteries and the attacking strategy was the most vociferous opponent of the attack taking place the next day.

The Chevalier D'Arcon was equally determined in his argument.

"Monsieur Le Duc, may I remind you that the floating batteries have been sailed here from France, that is the only sailing experience they or their crews have had, there has been no examination or trials on their capabilities under conditions of battle. If we attack tomorrow the floating batteries will go into battle for the first time without any of them having fired a single cannon ball from their decks before. I can carry on if you wish, I am pleading with you for at least 10 days to take the floating batteries out and properly test their sea worthiness and fighting capability"?

The two Spaniards had put national rivalries aside as they listened to the discussion, both men agreed with the Chevalier D'Arcon but for the same and their own reasons. Admiral Barcelo was mainly concerned for the lives of his sailors going into battle in untried ships for Admiral Moreno it was about reputation.

"Let me be clear Monsieur Le Duc, I will lead this attack if you so order; but I want it recorded what has been said in this meeting and that I pledge to lead the attack with all my ability but mine and the concerns of the other officers present has been duly noted by you", Moreno was making his own case.

The Prince of Nassau was the one person who had remained silent. The Prince like his two French counterparts was high born and considered somewhat of a rogue and womaniser but this aside he had years of Naval experience and his courage was never in doubt.

"Well, any observations from you Nassau"? Asked the Duc.

"No, monsieur it's all been said, let us get on with it, I relish any opportunity to close on the English and kill them".

This did raise a smile amongst all present and if anything improved the atmosphere in the room.

"So, Messieurs, I have noted your concerns but the attack will commence as planned tomorrow, I have 50 ships, 300 barges and 35,000 soldiers waiting for orders, we cannot keep them idle forever, we also have half of Spain here in Algeciras, I have two fears, disorder amongst the thousands here and a change in weather, once the storm season starts our naval options will be considerably reduced. I would add that some of most distinguished peers from Madrid and Paris are already here in Algeciras to see history take place, we must not disappoint them or the thousands camped on the hills. The attack will be led by you Admiral Moreno with the prince as your second in command".

Both men nodded assent.

The Duc then showed his ace card, "there is also another pressing matter; I have information that the British have another relief fleet on route to Gibraltar as we speak, so there you have it. Now go and make your preparations".

Glances were exchanged between all, that was it; the decision was final, as the commanders filed out of the room the Duc looked at the map and slammed the point end of the walking cane into the King's Bastion!

Everyone in Gibraltar, soldiers, sailors, and civilians knew that a major attack was imminent; they could see people gathering on the hills above Algeciras in their thousands, there was also so much activity on the enemy shore that Governor Elliot and his commanders could watch the allied preparations while standing on the King's Bastion.

Back at the Governor Generals building the mood was sombre as Governor Elliot addressed the assembled officers.

"Gentlemen, throughout this siege there has, I think you would agree, been an attitude of acceptance that the Spaniards can surround the Rock but would never get inside it. This time will be different, the first ever concerted attack is to happen and if the Spanish get inside our defences they will take their frustrations out on our soldiers and no doubt the civilian population after waiting 78 years to take back what was they see as rightfully theirs".

All of the officers understood Governor Elliot's meaning, 30,000 soldiers set loose in a piece of land a mile long would run amok and every person on the Rock would be put under the bayonet, there was real fear.

"Go back to your men and make it very clear to them that the usual rules of European warfare will not apply, this will be a fight to the death; there will be no surrender from us, I expect your men to expend every cartridge, every cannonball and when they are done they use their bayonets and musket butts, I will not surrender the Rock under any circumstances, are we clear gentlemen"?

"Sir, My Lord" echoed around the room.

"Good gentlemen, to your duties", Governor Elliot then did what he had done so many times before, he turned and looked out the window of his office towards Algeciras.

Every regiment in the garrison was stood to; ready to be deployed, the three Royal Navy ships assigned to the Rock and Governor Elliot's gunboats were also at battle stations. The whole atmosphere in Gibraltar was tense and depressed, like a ghost town, all the taverns were closed; Governor Elliot wanted every one of his garrison fit, sober and ready to their duty when the attack came.

Since the incident at the tavern Lara had been in a sombre mood. Lara knew what Campbell was about but she found it hard to reconcile herself that she had killed him; her mood wasn't helped by the fact that Tom had been prevented from seeing her ever since, restricted to his duties with his company. More than anything Lara felt lonely, the tavern was closed, there were no customers so she needed no help. There she sat in the empty tavern, rubbing the growing bump on her stomach, praying to god asking forgiveness for committing murder and pleading at the same time, "Holy Father, let my Thomas come through this battle I don't want to be alone with our child".

Barracks rooms are normally noisy places, banter, laughter, anger; always lively but not this time. The soldiers were kept busy drilling by their Officers and Sergeants, attending to their weapons and equipment. If anything, the soldiers welcomed the jobs given to them, it kept their minds occupied and at the same time they were ready for what was to come.

Tom's mood was no better than Lara's. Killing in battle was what he did as part of his army life, the death of Campbell however justified it may have been was wrong in his mind and like the other soldiers keeping himself busy was the only way to block out the images of Campbell bleeding to death in front of him. To this end, Tom had volunteered the Light Company of the 39th to work on the Kings Bastion keeping the gunners supplied with cannon balls and whatever they needed when the attack came. It also included guard and lookout duty on the same position. Although Tom and the officers knew what was coming; the floating batteries had been kept secret from the garrison as a whole. Governor Elliot was concerned about morale and didn't want the men giving up the fight before it started. Tom was also tired, the mission, the deaths, Hogan and McGann, everything. If the fight was to happen let it come soon; he wanted the whole thing over with and yes; he missed Lara.

Soldiers were not stupid though, they could see old houses in the town being pulled down and the scrap wood brought to the King's Bastion where there were a number of grates and ovens being set up by the gunners, this could only mean "Red Hot Shot", what was coming at them?

13th September 1782

The festival was finished in Algeciras. Like Gibraltar the taverns were closed. The whole town and thousands more had made their way to the hills above to sit and watch the day's events.

A grandstand had been built for the dignitaries from Madrid and Paris to sit and watch in comfort protected from the sun and the common people around them.

The port itself was all activity; thousands of troops were ready on standby to board the hundreds of transport barges. The whole allied fleet was at battle readiness and prepared to sail out from the port.

The main Spanish camp at Point Mala was also empty; the troops had made their way to behind the Spanish forward positions at the land crossing, they would wait until the time was right and the order was given for them to stream across the causeway into Gibraltar.

Like their British enemies they were all nervous, fiddling with their weapons and equipment to find something to do; each man praying he would wake to see the morning sun of the next day.

The floating batteries were as ready as they ever would be to sail into the battle. The Duc de Crillon stood on the Quayside with Admiral Moreno, Chevalier D'Arcon and the Prince of Nassau.

"Messieurs, the whole day rests on your ability to destroy the King's Bastion, when I receive your signal that this has been accomplished then the rest of the fleet and the landing barges will join the attack. I wish you all the luck of the day and pray god we will meet this evening in all good health".

Admiral Moreno was the first to respond, "thankyou Monsieur le Duc, Spain has waited long and hard for this day, I will press the attack hard, remember that when the signal is made for the fleet and assault troops to deploy I expect their best support".

"I assure you that you shall have it Admiral" answered the Duc.

At that all four men shook hands and made their farewells, Admiral Moreno boarding his 21 gun flagship, the Pastora, as second in command the Chevalier D'Arcon and the Prince of Nassau boarded the Talla Piedra, also boasting 21 guns.

It was early in the morning just after 7 o'clock with a mist floating across the bay that separated Algeciras and Gibraltar. Standing on the King's Bastion on lookout was Private Joseph Flynn of the 39th Foot Light Company. Leaning on his Brown Bess and looking out beyond the stone parapet to the sea in front. Soldiers, civilians all had been talking about the coming attack; Flynn was bored with such talk. The only thing Flynn was on the lookout for was a relief fleet, something that would lift the siege and get him off this mile long stretch of land and somewhere different.

The Kings Bastion had been fortified ready for the coming battle. Caissons of barrels filled with earth and wood had been added to the firing embrasures and the gunners of the Royal Artillery who would fire the British 24 pounder guns were also ready.

Minutes went by and Flynn's mind wandered as the morning mist started to lift and move away allowing him a clear view of the Mediterranean, how was he here and what was he doing all this way from Ireland; then he saw something.

Large, very large wooden shapes in a bent line; but moving in formation coming out of Algeciras. Flynn was frozen to the spot, he rubbed his eyes his eyes and looked again, they were coming.

"Sah, sah, Sergeant Sullivan, you need to come here Sergeant, now"! he muttered.

Tom was asleep on the battlement a few feet from Flynn, he sat up half asleep throwing his blanket off himself, "What is it Flynn" he asked as he woke up.

Flynn didn't answer and stared out towards sea; Tom jumped up and ran towards him. Tom recognised the shape of them straight away; the floating batteries had come to do their work. My god, Tom thought, they were impressive things to look at when he saw them at the quayside in Algeciras but at sea, they were awesome and magnificent at the same time.

"Fire your musket man and stand to now"! Tom barked at Flynn.

It was a relief for Flynn; he fired his Brown Bess and ran to the end of the rampart ringing the alarm bell shouting "Stand To" at the top of his voice.

Within minutes the King's Bastion was a frenzy of activity, officers, gunners, soldiers running to their positions and preparing their batteries. It was the same for the whole of the Rock, 5,000 men were now stood to ready to repel the allied attack.

Within 30 minutes Governor Elliot arrived at the King's Bastion with General Ross acknowledging Tom with a "Sullivan" as he positioned himself with a spy glass to view the approaching enemy ships. Governor Elliot looked at the floating batteries and then behind them to the hills above Algeciras and the throngs of people come to watch the grand attack.

"My god is that a grandstand they built there"? he laughed as he said it.

After handing the spy glass to General Ross, Governor Elliot turned to the Senior Artillery Officers on the Bastion, Colonel Green and Captain Koelher.

"Gentlemen, fire up the grates and ovens now, you both know what is to be done, once they take position bring every gun to bear on them, I want red hot shot poured onto those floating monsters, the fight is here right now, the success of this battle is on your shoulders, now do your duty".

"My lord" and both men were off giving orders and directing the preparations for the attack. Tom and his men were despatched to bring water and other supplies to the bastion in the short time available before the floating batteries were on them.

The progress of the floating batteries was slow and ponderous, inside the Pastora Admiral Moreno was becoming impatient, the Talla Piedra was with him but where were the other batteries? They were too far behind; the attack would only be successful if all 10 ships could bring their guns to bear on the Kings Bastion at the same time. Moreno looked at the crew, their captain, Lopez, they were doing their best for him for Spain, their lives were in his hands he would do his best for them.

Moreno used his spyglass to look at the Kings Bastion, "it appears the English can see us, the Kings Bastion has come alive, here look for yourself, passing the spyglass to Captain Lopez.

Lopez was young and keen, "yes, admiral when can we get at them"? Asked Lopez in anticipation.

Moreno looked at Lopez and his crew, "just as soon as I have all my ships in formation, then we will be the hammer that will smash this Kings Bastion into pieces once and for all, have the men take battle stations". The sailors cheered they were up for the fight.

The mood in the Talla Piedra was much the same. Chevalier D'Arcon was equally frustrated, why hadn't the Duc de Crillon taken his advice? The floating batteries were not able for difficult manoeuvres, it was too late now.

As ever the Prince of Nassau was calm and confident. "My dear Chevalier, this is where we are now, grinding your teeth will make no difference, the English are there", pointing at the Kings Bastion, "now let us prepare our men and ready ourselves to destroy the English defences, this day will be ours, of that I am sure".

The ship's captain was Mendoza; D'Arcon did not know him well but could see he was an experienced naval officer.

D'Arcon nodded," you have reason Nassau, yes, now let's get on with it, Captain Mendoza prepare your guns".

It was the order Mendoza and the ship's company has been waiting for, like their comrades on the Pastora they readied their 21 guns with gusto.

By about 9.30am the Pastora and Talla Piedra had anchored directly opposite the King's Bastion and dropped anchors, the others had bunched opposite the Old Mole, every gun on each floating battery was ready to fire.

Admiral Moreno used his spyglass to review the positions of the other floating batteries, he knew the formation of the attacking ships were as good as they would get under the conditions. He summoned Captain Lopez.

"I'm fearful of moving any further and losing position where we are, signal all the other ships, commence firing now"!

First the Pastora and Talla Piedra opened up on the Kings Bastion, then the 200 guns of the combined floating batteries fired almost all at the same time at the Old Mole, the "Grand Attack" had begun.

The soldiers at the Kings Bastion stared at the massive ships, almost rooted to the spot, at first they were scared by them. Captain Koehler noted the mood of the men, "heads up now lads, they're all just large lumps of wood, you're the best gunners in his majesty's army, now let's show them how good you are"

The men shouted "huzzah" in reply waiving their tricorns in the air.

The cheering was short lived, they saw the fireballs then heard the noise from the floating batteries, the shout of "take cover" went along the line; they knew the first volley would be the most dangerous. Men dropped down to the ground, others crouched behind the constructed ballast, heads around their hands and ears.

Crash, cannonballs smashed into the bastion, men were thrown off battlements by the force of the shot, one after another more direct hits on the Kings Bastion, men were hugging the floor trying to burrow themselves into the stone structure praying for the never-ending salvo to finish.

Almost as soon it began the first barrage from the floating batteries was over, there was the noise of men coughing, wounded, moaning then the shouts of Sergeants, officers, they had survived; the Kings Bastion was sturdy and held up well against the allied fire.

Colonel Green and Captain Koehler made themselves as visible as possible to their men walking up and down the bastion shouting, "right men were still here, get up, it's our turn", gunners got up dusted themselves off and took position at their cannons.

Within a minute every cannon on the King's Bastion was ready to fire, Colonel Green nodded to Captain Koehler, "fire", the men of the Royal Artillery had been waiting for this moment as they delivered a score of cannonballs at the floating batteries.

Inside the Pastora Captain Lopez put down his spy glass as he saw the flashes and fireballs from the Kings Bastion, "prepare to take fire" he shouted. Sailors made the sign of the cross and then there were bangs and booms as the English cannonballs hit the ship, men were jolted and staggered back but looked around in amazement and the strangest noise; cannonballs bouncing off the Pastora and drooping into the sea! No flying splinters, no cannon balls ripping through them, the extra planking was working! The men cheered and looked to Admiral Moreno and Captain Lopez. Captain Lopez seized the moment, "you see men, they can't hurt us now keep on firing"! More cheering and the sailors set about reloading their guns.

On the Kings Bastion Captain Koehler could hardly believe his eyes as he put his spy glass down, "now I've seen everything; our cannon balls are bouncing off their hulls"!

Colonel Green had seen the same spectacle almost admiring the ingenuity of the allied naval engineers; he called over Koehler and the Master Gunnery Sergeant. Despite the noise of his guns and the crashing of cannonballs hitting the bastion he was in control.

"Well we can't stand here and let them fire at us at will, put every gun to them with normal shot, it seems they're not moving, adjust your cannon, aim at the gun ports and their sails, if we hit them they'll be sure to feel it; what is the progress with the grates"?.

"Still not hot enough Colonel", answered the Gunnery Sergeant.

"Then pull more buildings down if you need to for firewood, in the meantime we'll disable their guns and their sails but I need that red hot shot"! Glaring at the Gunnery Sergeant as he said so.

The Kings Bastion may have been fortified ready for the Grand Attack but Gibraltar Town was not. The Spanish opened up from their forward trenches on the land crossing with every gun, cannonballs rained down on the Grand Parade inside the Rock itself. People, redcoats, everyone ran to take cover wherever they could. Inside the tavern; Lara was hiding under a table as she could hear the town being smashed to pieces around her. She held her hands over her ears, the screaming of the Spanish shots, the crash as they hit the buildings, it was too much, she thought she would die this would be her just punishment for killing another human being, she didn't care for herself; as tears ran down her face she prayed," Holy father take me but protect my Thomas and my child".

For now the battle was on with both sides fully committed. Cannonballs rained forward and backwards between the floating batteries and the Kings Bastion for several hours, neither could see the damage they were causing to each other so they carried on firing relentlessly but men were being killed and wounded on both sides.

Tom and his men had been busy carrying ordnance to the gunners and running back to the magazine below the bastion to fetch more. They were grabbing more supplies inside the magazine when they heard and felt a tremendous crash. They ran outside into the main yard and saw a gun on the bastion had taken a direct hit, the embrasure was destroyed and the gun crew were dead or maimed. Tom paused for one moment, his mind was taking in more death, his men looked to him.

"Sergeant, what do we do, tend the gunners or carry ordnance", asked a private.

The question shook him back to life, "No! Carry on supplying the gunners".

The men carried on with their duty and Tom shouted for stretcher bearers all the while thinking how much more of this attack could the bastion or the whole Rock for that matter endure?

Admiral Moreno was becoming nervous, the floating batteries were hitting the Kings Bastion but between the clouds of smoke he could see no let-up in the enemy's resistance. Several of his own guns had been hit and put of action by the English gunners and the euphoria of earlier was replaced by the groans of dying men. He was also conscious that two of the Pastora's masts had been brought down, it was taking too much fire; he turned to Captain Lopez.

"Captain Lopez, are we able to move forwards to limit the effect of their guns and adjust our fire into their flanks"?

Lopez was nervous then answered, "My lord, it is impossible; the ship is touching the seabed we cannot move"!

Moreno was incredulous, "My god, what has De Crillon done to us? Captain, send messages to the other ships, behind the Talla Pedra, I want the Paula Prima, El Rosario and the San Cristobal to sail ahead of us and fire into the flanks of the Kings Bastion, do it now"!

Messages were sent by rowing boat and signal flags to the three ships, they all came back with the same reply as that from the Talla

Piedra and the other floating batteries, they were also unable to manoeuvre!

Inside the Talla Piedra the situation was becoming desperate, Chevalier D'Arcon had removed his tunic; the heat was incredible, the smoke of the guns and an enclosed deck made the conditions on the warship as hot as a boiling cauldron. Wounded men were everywhere, sailors were also collapsing because of the heat, they could hardly breathe. The Chevalier D'Arcon watched as yet another cannon was blown from its carriage, wrecking it completely and killing most of the gun crew.

"Bastard English" he swore as exhausted medical orderlies ran to the wounded men.

Like everyone inside the Talla Piedra the Prince of Nassau was coated in a mixture of dark dried sweat and smoke but he remained calm as ever in front of his men.

"Yes Chevalier, they can see we cannot move in either direction so their gunners are concentrating on our sails and our guns; of which we started with 21 and 8 have now been destroyed, not to mention our sails all shot down, I pray Moreno calls for the combined fleet to sail or we are finished here"!

The Chevalier was incandescent with anger, "I told de Crillon, I told him, we needed more time but he wouldn't listen, now look at us"!

"Anger will come later, for now we must attend to our duty and our men" answered the Prince as he turned his head to survey the scene of carnage inside the Talla Piedra.

On the Kings Bastion the defenders were becoming more confident. Their fortifications were holding up against the fire of the floating batteries and if anything the rate of fire they were receiving was slowing down. Before long it became clear to Captain Koehler the predicament the attacking ships were in, "why are they just sitting there; Is it because they are stuck"? He said turning to Colonel Green.

Green answered still looking through his spy glass, "I'm no sailor Captain, get a Royal Navy Officer up here right away then we'll know sure enough.

Within Minutes a Royal Navy officer was on the Kings Bastion, after some minutes he snapped his spy glass shut.

"It would appear our Spanish foes have been foolish; they should have sent one of their floating monsters in to test the waters, they are particularly shallow there. There can be no other reason gentlemen, why else would they sit there like sitting ducks, between their masts being blown away by your guns and the seabed they can' t move, you may place your shots at will"!

It had taken ages to heat up the cannon balls into red hot shot but by midday they were ready just as Governor Elliot appeared again on the Kings Bastion.

"Well gentlemen, what are they doing", he asked as he looked at the floating batteries through his spy glass.

"They are still holding my Lord, but they are stuck and we are hitting their guns and sails", answered Colonel Green.

"If they want some more then give them more", Governor Elliot snapped his spy glass shut looking at his officers.

"Indeed my lord, I am informed the red hot shot is ready".

"Good, then look at those two", pointing at the Pastora and the Talla Piedra.

"There, those two ships they are clearly their flagships, concentrate your fire on them, if we stop them we stop them all"!

Within minutes Tom and his men were lifting the red hot cannonballs on steel rods up to the parapets where the gunners were, the heat coming off them was so intense they wore kerchiefs around their faces and cloths around their hands to protect their skin.

As the first salvos of red hot shot were fired by the Royal Artillery just standing near the guns was almost unbearable because of the powerful heat coming off the grates.

The sailors inside the floating batteries felt the difference as the red hot shot hit their ships, the noise, the sizzling thud, the flames, they were now terrified!

Not just flames from the British guns, flames were coming at them, like comets! Captain Lopez pointed towards the Kings Bastion, "No more cannonballs they are hitting us with red hot shot, look Admiral"!

Admiral Moreno was resigned to the situation and hurriedly wrote a note handing it to Captain Lopez.

"It is only a matter of time before they will have us on fire, we cannot manoeuvre these hulks, we must have the combined fleet to join us and put fire onto the bastion, send a messenger now, with these words, we must have support now"!

Captain Lopez summoned a sailor handing him the message and sending him on his way.

Cannonballs from the Spanish land batteries still fell on the town, every one hid wherever they could but houses were getting smashed and flattened, Lara covered her ears hiding under the table her only protection, when would it end, she could her the thuds and the explosion close by, the deadly whistle of the shot as it got closer, too close!

Tom and his men lost count of how many burning hot grates of shot they carried up to the gun batteries. Smoke, there was nothing but smoke between the Kings Bastion and the floating batteries, broken only by the fireballs between each cannon British or Spanish as they fired. Redcoats, not any more, all of Toms uniform was black, tunic, leggings everything, their faces covered in dry, acrid smoke, their throats parched, eyes stinging, but still they carried more shots and still the gunners poured it onto the floating batteries.

Every time Tom got up on the Bastion he craned his neck and strained his eyes looking towards the two flagships, when would the fire from the red hot shot take effect?

He saw something through the smoke, flames, small at first and then bigger, the Talla Piedra was on fire!

"Look Sergeant its working, the first battery is on fire"! Tom shouted towards the Master Gunnery Sergeant. They were joined by Captain Koehler and Colonel Green.

Spy glasses went up along the bastion.

"By god we have them, we have them; keep that shot coming they're on fire alright". Colonel Green shouted

Officers, soldiers, gunners , everyone on the bastion shouted in celebration, the gunners needed no further encouragement, they kept pouring red hot shots onto the hulks, the hulks just sat there not moving, everyone cannon ball from the Kings Bastion hit their targets, the gunners had their range perfect!

The people sat on the hills of Algeciras not hundreds but thousands, 80,000 by any reckoning. Where was the victory? This was what they had come to see.

The Duc de Crillon had kept his distance from the grandstand; he didn't want to deal with ridiculous questions or suggestions from the good and the great. Then the message arrived from Admiral Moreno pleading with him to deploy the combined fleet.

The message read," Monsieur Le Duc, the British are using red shot against us, my ship is on fire and the other batteries will suffer the same fate soon. Half of my men are dead or disabled as are my guns and sails, we cannot move from our position. Unless you send the combined fleet at all speed to support us, we, and all the batteries are doomed, Admiral Moreno".

The Duc de Crillon, Admiral Barcelo and the other commanders watched the attack and read the message, "send the fleet, we haven't breached the defences, where would we put them? This would be a disaster, no, the fleet will hold until we see the guns on the Kings Bastion silenced and the defences breached".

Admiral Barcelo walked away, "where are you going Barcelo there is still duty to perform" asked De Crillon.

"You will pardon me Monsieur Le Duc, I will always perform my duty with the utmost integrity and honour; but sitting on my backside watching my men being slaughtered, that I cannot do".

As the allied commanders turned back to look at the battle the silence amongst them was deafening.

The heat was unbearable inside the floating batteries, the noise was equally devastating, with an enclosed deck the roar of the cannons had nowhere to go, for the allied commanders they had difficulty communicating with their own crews never mind the other 8 ships in their flotilla. Admiral Moreno was on his knees, holding the hand of Captain Lopez. Lopez was dying in front of his eyes; a smashed wood splinter lodged in his chest, despite his agony Lopez could think only of his men. "Admiral I beg you look to my brave men, they have given their best for Spain this day".

Moreno could barely contain himself, he squeezed Lopez's hand tighter, "Have no fear captain, I will see to the men, now and always; believe me there's none braver than you".

Lopez was calmed by Moreno's words and as his grip on the Admiral's hand loosened so he passed on to the next world. Admiral Moreno made the sign of the cross on the dead man's cheek and said the "Our Father". As he walked away to continue with the battle, he could only think that the he and all the men on the floating batteries had been betrayed and consigned to doom by their commanders.

Sure enough the red hot shot took effect on all the floating batteries; fire set on the Talla Piedra, the Pastora and then the others. Spanish and French sailors risked their lives climbing onto the hulls of their ships trying to put the fires out with cloths and buckets of water but it was no use; the red hot cannon balls had lodged into the wood of the hulls where they hit and the fire spread around them.

The situation on the Talla Piedra was just as bad as that of the Pastora, they had been in constant battle with the Kings Bastion for eight hours and of their original 21 guns only 5 were capable of being fired. The Prince of Nassau had taken direct command of the ship; Captain Mendoza was dead, killed by British cannon fire from the Kings Bastion.

Chevalier D'Arcon and the Prince of Nassau knew that the end was near.

The Prince addressed one of the few officers not dead or maimed on the Pastora.

"It would appear we are on fire, pour water on the last of our gunpowder now, before the whole ship blows and send word to Admiral Moreno that we are abandoning ship".

As the order was given, D'Arcon said nothing and the battle weary crew dropped their heads in pure misery.

Admiral Moreno received the news that the combined fleet would not put to sea. As he surveyed the scene around him he could see the flames on the Talla Piedra and the same on the other batteries. Moreno had made his decision.

He turned to an officer," send the signal to all ships, fire your ships and save your men, I would rather see them burn than let the English have them"!

Boats set sail from Algeciras to try to rescue the men of the floating batteries but there were nowhere near enough of them. Admiral Moreno was true to his word for Lopez, he did his best to get every man onto the rescue boats, those that could move and he was last off the Pastora as more flames engulfed it.

On the Talla Piedra, those sailors that were able; climbed down onto the boats, the wounded and others were still on board, Chevalier D'Arcon climbed down into a boat but he was alone, he turned back and saw the prince of Nassau standing on the top of the ship, what was he doing?

Chevalier D'Arcon shouted back, "don't be a fool, get on the boat Nassau"

"I would love to Chevalier but I have a pressing need, to stay with my men, they have need of me, god be with you", he then turned and climbed back inside the Talla Piedra.

It was almost midnight, the battle had raged for over 14 hours, the men of the Kings Bastion rested for the first time since the opening volley from the floating batteries earlier that morning, no one spoke; they had stopped firing there was nothing left to fire at except burning ships and floating bodies. This was it, the "Grand Attack", the great effort by the Spanish and their French allies to destroy the defences of Gibraltar and they had broken it, in themselves every soldier standing on the Kings Bastion knew they had broken the siege.

When Tom was a child in Tipperary Father Ryan told them of Dante's Inferno; a vision of hell. Looking into the bay that was what he could see. Burning and sinking ships, dead bodies floating in their masses, many a brave man died that day, there was relief they had broken the attack but no joyous celebrations, one doesn't celebrate looking at misery of that sort. As a man Tom felt he was no longer scared of going to hell; it was there in front of his eyes.

They watched as the fire on each floating battery took its toll and they started to explode, break up and then sink.

Colonel Green broke the silence, "Men, the battle is won, now I need volunteers now to rescue survivors from those hulks", every man on the Kings Bastion raised his arm to volunteer.

They set out on Governor Elliot's gunboats and anything that would float from the Old Mole, waving white flags towards the Spanish shore guns, the firing ceased.

Each allied sailor pulled from the water was either burnt or wounded in some way and for Tom and the others again these men stopped being the enemy and became human beings.

The allied losses were horrendous with the dead and drowned floating face down in the sea. Those that lived held on to broken pieces of their once proud ships waving their arms at the unlikely saviours wearing red. Eager arms reached out from the rescue boats pulling the allied sailors on board and out of danger. Tom and his men were in the rescue boats and they worked tirelessly for several hours doing the best for their once enemies. They wanted to do more but had to go back to the Old Mole as some of the last floating batteries were in danger of blowing up. The survivors and wounded were taken into the town from the Old Mole, they were completely broken; surgeons and stretcher bearers arrived and did their best for them.

Admiral Moreno and Chevalier D'Arcon sat in a rescue boat full of wounded sailors that made its way back to Algeciras leaving the flames of the burning floating batteries behind them. It was pure and utter misery, the groans of the wounded men, neither man could speak, their faces black from smoke and gun powder, their once fine uniforms in tatters, their attack had failed but worse than that they felt betrayed by their own commanders. The Prince of Nassau had died on the Talla Piedra with his men; a part of them wished they had done the same.

It was 5 o'clock in the morning, the crowds on the hill had left many hours before and the grandstand of dignitaries was empty. The Duc de Crillon put down his spyglass after surveying the same vision of hell, he turned to the nearest officer, "stand the men down, its over".

As the assembled officers walked away in silence, the Duc looked at the empty grandstand where the dignitaries once sat, where were they now? He thought. The first explanations of his failure would begin at once.

Their duty done Tom paraded his men back on the Kings Bastion; they had done their duty for nearly 24 hours but incredibly had not lost a single man. In fact, for the Gibraltar Garrison their losses were less than 20 men killed in the whole battle.

Just then, Governor Elliot and his entourage appeared on the Bastion to the cheers and hurrahs of all, he addressed the assembled troops.

"Men we have broken them, this was their grand attack, we have withstood and destroyed their floating batteries, there is nothing else for them now, you have fought bravely this long day and night. His Majesty will be proud of you, go now and rest and remember in years to come when people talk of the grand attack at Gibraltar; you are some of the few who can say, I was there"!

This time the cheer was even louder as the Governor went to leave; seeing Tom he stopped.

"Bunker Hill, you were right Sullivan, find your position, fortify and concentrate your fire".

"My Lord", Tom stood to attention, a wry smile on his face.

With the men dismissed there was only one place he was going. Not realising it; he was running as fast as his legs could carry him.

As he ran through the streets, debris from the buildings hit by the Spanish land batteries was everywhere, he was exhausted but he found the spirit in his tired limbs to keep running.

"Please god let her live", he prayed to himself as he ran through the destroyed houses in the Grand Parade. Then he saw it, the tavern was still standing it hadn't been touched, the buildings either side of it had been smashed to smithereens but there stood the tavern as though the hand of god had covered it and protected it from the cannonballs.

He ran through the door smashing it open, where was she? He looked all around, tables were turned over, there was dust everywhere, he stopped, panting, out of breath.

Then he heard sniffling, where? He looked to the corner and there she was, Lara, sitting on the floor crying, legs cradled up against her chest, she was alive!

He ran across and picked her up and they held each other, it was over, and they were together again.

They had come through it; they would never be apart again!

Chapter 6
The Greatest Loss

There was a ceasefire, not official but it was a ceasefire; both sides were exhausted they had nothing left to give and the siege was at a standstill. The Allied force couldn't get into Gibraltar and the British couldn't get out.

In October the relief fleet under Admiral Rodney of 34 Royal Navy ships of the line and an equal number of ships carrying supplies avoided the allied fleet and slipped into Gibraltar. The ships brought food, ammunition and 2,000 more soldiers as reinforcements, it was clear to the allies and the British that the Rock would not fall.

The daily artillery contest between the Spanish forward lines and Willis' carried on as normal but apart from this there was no offensive or defensive ambition from either side. For the Spanish and French they knew there would be no further action like the "Grand Attack" and for the British it was a case of waiting for a settlement to be reached that would bring the siege to an end.

Christmas came and went and in the February of the year 1783 Lara gave birth to a healthy baby boy.

For Tom Sullivan his joy in holding the child was inexpressible. It truly was a wonder for him and his life had true meaning; he named the child Joseph James after his two brothers. For Lara, she truly had her man and she had his baby as well. Tom loved that boy so much; he loved Lara the same.

Tom was emotional and thought of his brothers, of little Maggie, his father; he hadn't written to them in years. How had his life run by him like this?

He promised himself he would change things. Tom told Lara he would leave the army and perhaps settle with her in Gibraltar things would get better.

Tom wanted no more war, no more death, he would stay there in Gibraltar and lived out his days like Tom Nugent back in Tipperary and raise his family with his wife and maybe more children. Tom's life could not be any better but circumstances thwarted his plans.

One morning a week the 39th Regiment of Foot would be paraded in full, all 600 officers and soldiers. Colonel Dachenhausen addressed the regiment.

"Sergeant Sullivan march forward".

Tom was completely startled and after an initial falter broke ranks and marched into the centre of the parade in front of the Colonel.

"Sergeant Sullivan, for your fine work in recent months and the leadership and gallantry you have shown in command of your men and on the recommendations of the Governor General you are promoted to Sergeant Major, I congratulate you".

Tom was astounded and accepted the promotion with satisfaction and surprise. Stepping forward he accepted a sword and a red sash from the Colonel, perhaps he would have to stay in the army for the time being.

That evening in the tavern the atmosphere was the best it had been in ages; packed full of soldiers drinking to Sergeant Major Sullivan's health. The men were pleased for Tom, the likes of Duggan and Murtagh who had served with him for years and the young boys he had brought through the siege. Lara was blooming, serving the men ale and cuddling Joseph James with her serving girls flirting with the men and playing with the child at the same time. Tom felt good and drunk some but not much; as a child in Tipperary he had seen drunkenness and he didn't care for it, he stepped outside the tavern to take some air.

"Sergeant Major Sullivan, congratulations on your promotion".

Tom turned to see the Provost Officer, Colonel Murray, smiling at him and immediately stood to attention with a, "Colonel".

"You may take your ease Sergeant Major, I have come to return this to you", handing Tom the small pistol he had given to Lara that killed Campbell; Tom did his best to appear calm and unknowing what it was about.

"I don't know what this is for Colonel"? Attempting to hand the pistol back as though it had nothing to do with him.

"I understand that you and the late Sergeant Campbell had some history, fighting in Dublin all those years ago, fighting here over your woman there inside the tavern, am I correct"? Colonel Murray was completely in charge of the conversation and Tom had no idea what is was leading to, was he to be placed under close arrest?

"That is true Colonel, we had our disagreements but the most I ever did was bash him about, nothing else", admit nothing he thought and protect Lara whatever the cost to himself.

"Sergeant Major, I am not here to place you under arrest but listen to me closely. I served in the American colonies as well and I recognise the pistol that was found near Campbell's body, a very careless act by the killer wouldn't you say Sergeant Major"? The Provost Officer leaned in very close to Tom.

"Colonel, with respect what is your point"? It was all or nothing now.

"That's better Sergeant Major, this is my point, I know Campbell was no good and I know something happened between you and him. Your reputation has served you well Sullivan, I could have investigated this further if I wanted to but I haven't. However, I warn you the next Provost Officer may not be as reasonable as me. There is a procedure in military discipline for dealing with the Campbell's of this world; if we ignore that and take the law into our hands then we would have chaos, would you agree"?

"Yes, Colonel I would agree", replied Tom.

"Good then I congratulate you again on your promotion and on the birth of your child but mark my words well Sergeant Major, I bid you good evening".

Colonel Murray turned and walked away before Tom could reply; he leaned back against the tavern door and took a deep breath; he walked back inside to rejoin Lara and his comrades, maybe he would drink more than usual this evening.

In March the ceasefire became official. Governor Elliot met with the Allied commanders and the daily artillery duels ceased.

It was agreed that prisoners would be exchanged and under a white flag, Tom and a company of the 39th marched the prisoners from the "Grand Attack" back to the Spanish forward lines on the causeway. Tom and his men felt exposed standing out in the open as the prisoners walked forward to the calls of the Spanish soldiers beckoning them towards them.

"Right lads, were done here, back to our lines now", Tom ordered the company of soldiers.

A shout came from the Spanish, "English wait, we have something for you"!

A solitary figure walked out from the Spanish trenches, he was wearing the clothes of a civilian and was limping, he had no uniform, who was it?

The man got closer. Tom and the other men recognised the figure, were they looking at a ghost? The face was scarred but the man was alive, it was Private Hogan!

The men gathered around Hogan, slapping him on the back, cheering and carrying him back on their shoulders to the British forward positions.

Once back, Hogan was sat down drinking Rum from a tankard with Major Kellet and Tom waiting for his story.

"So Hogan, how are you alive"? Asked the Major.

"As you can see from my face Major, they beat me to a pulp; I couldn't tell them any more than my regiment and name because my mouth had swollen so much and I collapsed. They were going to hang me but changed their mind after the attack of the floating batteries. My guard told me that they saw British boats going out to rescue their men from the sea after the attack had failed and decided to keep me a prisoner, that's all I know".

"Well Hogan, that's as good a reason as any, whatever the case you are alive, the surgeon is waiting to examine you, we can talk again later".

At that, Hogan was taken to the surgeon and Tom Sullivan felt contentment in his soul. A child, a promotion, the Campbell business resolved and now a man whom he thought had died under his wing was alive; life was good at this moment.

It was a beautiful morning in March but Captain Antonio Lopez was drunk and everyday he drunk more to forget the misery in his mind. Lopez had served in the Spanish forward positions for over 3 years and the nearest he had got to the British was when they came and raided their positions destroying them in the mass sortie. Lopez knew the ceasefire was a prelude to a full cessation of hostilities; this meant that Spain had failed again to reconquer Gibraltar. Lopez was also bitter because his brother Miguel had died serving on the Pastora as captain in the "Grand Attack" with Admiral Moreno. Frustration, defeat and personal loss; he drunk more wine from an emptying bottle and sent his men away to the rear trench to collect supplies that were not needed. This day he would have his personal revenge on the English.

Sergeant Major Tom Sullivan was serving in the British lines directly across the causeway from Lopez. Tom's mind was not on his work, there was a ceasefire, it was a matter of time before the siege was over; his only thoughts were to finish his hours and see Lara and his son.

Lara decided to surprise Tom. Leaving Joseph James with the girls at the tavern she put some bread and cheese in a basket and thought she would meet him at the forward lines to eat together. Why not, Tom was now a Sergeant Major and there was no more fighting going on.

Lopez had the trench all to himself, an experienced soldier he loaded a cannon without any problem. This will be the last shot of the siege he thought to himself. The English would not be expecting any fire to come their way, they would be caught off guard and he would kill some of them.

Lara strolled towards the forward lines; she looked up at the blue Mediterranean sky and thought how beautiful the day was and how happy her life was. It didn't take long before she reached a wooden guard building and there he was. Tom was leaning over the sandbag barrier looking towards the Spanish, Willie Duggan was beside him.

"My Thomas, it's me", she called in her beautiful lilting accent.

The Cannon was ready and Lopez put the red hot iron to the ignition powder, "this is for my brother", he drunkenly slurred.

Bang! The cannon fired.

It was as though Tom heard Lara's voice and the Spanish cannon fire at the same time, he turned to her and screamed, "Lara, get down"!

Lara smiled at him and stood still where she was; as though she knew what was to happen.

Just like the explosion at Willis' Tom knew this was bad when he heard the report of the shot and the cannon ball. Time stood still as he looked at Lara smiling at him.

The guard building took a direct hit from the cannonball and exploded into bits sending Lara flying.

Lopez slumped over the cannon laughing, soldiers ran from all over the Spanish trenches towards his position. As the soldiers reached him, Lopez saluted them and said, "Adios Amigos", he then put his officer's pistol in his mouth and pulled the trigger.

Tom and the men pulled at the debris with their bare hands, broken bricks, wood, everything was thrown aside, then he saw her legs protruding from under a large wooden board, they were smashed in the most awful way, they removed the board, Lara was alive, just.

Tom put his hands on her shoulders, he held her hand; there were screams behind him, "get a surgeon here now"!

Lara was dying and both she and Tom knew it.

"Let me feel your hand on my face, one more time my Thomas", he put his hand on her face.

"I love you so much my Thomas, never forget this, never forget me, pray for me and look after Joseph James, our child, when I meet Jesus, I will tell him what a good man you are". Tears rolled down the sides of her face but she seemed at peace.

"I will never forget you Lara and I promise you Joseph James will be safe with me", he was crying but he didn't realise it.

The surgeon arrived and almost as quickly looked at Tom and shook his head, he walked away.

Tom leaned down to hug Lara one more time, he kissed and squeezed her gently, when he moved back up she was dead.

Tom was in pieces and was pulled from her by Duggan and the boys, "Tom, let us do right by her", Lara was gone and so was Gibraltar for Tom Sullivan.

Three weeks later, the peace was official and the siege was over; Tom found himself again standing again in front of Governor Elliot's desk.

"I heard about your woman Sullivan, I am sorry indeed, how are you"?

"It has been a difficult time my lord but Major Kellet has kept me occupied". Tom answered; he was gaunt and looked tired.

"I have no doubt Sergeant Major, the very reason why you are here now. Your regiment will stay in Gibraltar for the time being. You have proved yourself to be a resourceful soldier who can be trusted to complete missions whatever the danger", the Governor paused.

"How can I help you my lord"? Tom was interested in something for the first time since Lara's death.

"The army has work for you, there is an assignment that must be done that requires a soldier of your skills and experience. You will first have to return to England, I cannot discuss the details now, what do you say Sullivan"?

"My answer is yes my lord", he couldn't wait to leave Gibraltar.

Tom kissed and hugged baby Joseph James then handed him back to one of Lara's serving girls from the tavern. He gave her a small bag full of coin but knew she could be trusted to look after his son until he returned to take him. Tom then turned to look at the Tavern one more time before he walked down to the harbour.

HMS Thetis sailed out of Gibraltar with the morning tide into the Mediterranean. As Tom looked back towards the "Rock", he missed his son already but he was glad to leave. After Lara's death he couldn't stay in Gibraltar; it was a town of ghosts for him; everywhere he looked he asked himself inside where was the woman he loved? He would return again but only to take his son away with him. As the ship sailed away the rock of Gibraltar got smaller and smaller then it was gone.

Authors Note

As the first major battle of the American War of Independence; Bunker Hill was a British victory but at a terrible cost. Of the 3,000 British troops who took part in the battle they sustained over a 1,000 men killed and wounded; a casualty rate of 1 in 3. The battle changed the whole attitude of the British Generals and troops towards their colonial foes. It proved that inexperienced militia men were willing and able to stand against regular British army troops in a pitched battle.

In Sullivan's War there were 2 assaults on the militia positions, in the real battle there was in fact 3. The 39th Regiment of Foot did not fight at Bunker Hill or serve in the American War of Independence.

General Joseph Warren did die in the battle but was killed by a musket ball not a bayonet, who delivered the killing shot is not known.

During the siege of Gibraltar the 39th Regiment of Foot served at the "Rock" with distinction throughout the whole siege but it was not present at the battle of Minden. The Prince of Nassau did serve on the Talla Piedra during the "Grand Attack" and in real life survived the battle. Where these historical inaccuracies occur; the author apologises but hopes the spirit of the history in the story contributed to an enjoyable read.

It is well known that the American War of Independence was a political and military defeat for Britain. The successful defence of Gibraltar was a significant British victory at a time when its influence elsewhere in the world was under pressure. In history, the siege should be remembered at three years and seven months as the longest ever siege endured by British armed forces. Importantly, for those keen on reading military history; the defence of Gibraltar is an abiding lesson in defence, planning and logistics that can we can learn from to this very day.

As for Sergeant Major Tom Sullivan; Governor Elliot and the British Army has more work for him.

Andy Clancy
November 2015

Lightning Source UK Ltd.
Milton Keynes UK
UKOW06f0634100616

275958UK00001B/89/P